# The Quest to Save Swindon

## Chapter One

The Amazing Frog stood atop the highest building in central Swindon. The sun had just risen over the horizon. The wind whipped past his tiny frog earholes. The Amazing Frog looked down at the beautiful landscape that spread out before him.

OK, mostly he just looked at the cars.

He wanted to jump on them so, so badly. Jumping from car to car was one of the Amazing Frog's favorite things. It was how he liked to start each day. Nothing much was better than careening through the air, bouncing from hood to hood, and smashing one car after another. Sometimes he even used trampolines and cannons to enhance his jumps and smashings.

In some cities, this sort of behavior might have been frowned on. But not in Swindon. The Amazing Frog's leaps were a point of pride for the local citizens. The Frog Police didn't even seem to mind. They only watched in awe as the Amazing Frog careened through the air each morning.

The Amazing Frog had a big day ahead of him. He would start by jumping on some cars. That was a given. But he would also pick up some trash, maybe go to a café and enjoy a Croak Zero—his favorite drink—and then journey by cannon over to the coastline to see his old pal Pig Newton. And once they were together? Who knew what exciting adventures they might get into.

The Amazing Frog selected a good-looking car on the ground far below him and prepared to jump. It was a bright red sedan that had been freshly painted and waxed. He couldn't wait to see how it felt when he was smashing it underneath his webbed froggy feet.

The Amazing Frog prepared to jump. Sometimes, he even did a countdown to make it more exciting.

"Three. . ." he began. "Two. . ."

But the Amazing Frog stopped before he got to one.

Something far away, on the edge of the horizon, had made him hesitate. It was tiny and pink, but it was getting larger by the moment. Soon it grew close enough to appear oblong and decidedly pig-shaped.

It was the Amazing Frog's old pal—and sometimes his means of transportation—Pig Newton. But this was very strange! Why was Pig Newton coming into the city? Like most pigs, Pig Newton normally preferred the countryside where there were lots of delicious scraps to eat, and you could easily make a mud puddle and roll around in it. (It was a lot harder to make a mud puddle in the city, because all the streets were paved.)

As Pig Newton grew closer, he sniffed the air like he was looking for something. His beady pig eyes anxiously scanned the horizon. The Amazing Frog realized that *he* might be just what Pig Newton was here to find.

The Amazing Frog dove off the side of the building. He did not land on a car, but rather in the dead center of an empty street. He flopped around for a moment, and then stood back up. Falling several stories might have meant the end of most frogs, but not the Amazing Frog. His ability to leap from tall structures and land safe-and-sound was just one of the many reasons he was so very amazing!

No sooner was the Amazing Frog back on his feet than Pig Newton walked around the corner. He seemed troubled, but a look of relief settled over his face when his eyes found the Amazing Frog. He quickly trotted over.

"Pig Newton?" said the Amazing Frog. "What are *you* doing *here*? I thought we weren't supposed to hang out until later in the afternoon."

"I need your help," Pig Newton replied nervously.

The Amazing Frog sighed. People were always asking for his help with things. He didn't always understand why. Sure, he could jump around and fly through the air and have adventures. But why this meant he was supposed to be good at solving people's mysteries was always confusing to him. Even so, he had learned to accept it.

"What's the problem?" the Amazing Frog asked.

"It's Pig Girl!" replied Pig Newton.

"Oh?" said the Amazing Frog. "What's wrong with her? Did you take her favorite wallowing spot again, and now she's mad? Because if you take another pig's favorite wallowing spot—where the mud is all nice and cool and squishy—then of course they're going to be really annoyed with you."

"No, no, no," said Pig Newton, shaking his head back and forth. "Nothing like that. The problem with Pig Girl is that I can't find her. Anywhere! We were supposed to have breakfast together this morning, but she never showed up! I've looked in all the places she normally hangs out, plus some of the places she doesn't. I looked under rocks and inside caves. I looked in the water and I looked on land. She's nowhere to be found!"

"Hmm," said the Amazing Frog. "That *is* very strange. Are you *sure* you looked everywhere?"

"Yes," said Pig Newton. "I'm totally sure."

"I see," said the Amazing Frog. "And have you told anybody else about this?"

Pig Newton shook his head No.

"In that case, we should probably start by going to the Frog Police," said the Amazing Frog. "That's always a sensible first step. We can file a missing persons report. I mean, a missing *pig* report. It's like a missing persons report . . . but for pigs."

"Will the Frog Police know what to do?" Pig Newton asked skeptically. "I get the feeling that they spend most of their time running around the city and indiscriminately chasing random frog criminals all day."

"You've got a point," said the Amazing Frog. "But I still think it's our best option."

"Fine," said Pig Newton with a sigh. "We'll do it your way. Do you want a ride?"

"I think you already know the answer to that question," the Amazing Frog said.

Without further ado, he leapt into the air and landed on Pig Newton's back, straddling him like a horse.

"Mush," said the Amazing Frog.

"I wish you wouldn't say that," moaned Pig Newton, beginning to trek in the direction of the police station. "People haven't said 'mush' in like 200 years. Except maybe to sled dogs. And I'm not a sled dog."

"What should I say when I'm riding a pig," the Amazing Frog asked.

"How about instead of mush, you say mud," said Pig Newton. "Because pigs like mud. A lot. Mush just sounds gross. Like something you have to eat if you've been a bad little kid."

"All right—I can do that," said the Amazing Frog. "To the police station! Mud!"

*"Where?!"* said Pig Newton. "I *love* mud!"

"I was just saying it because you told me to. . . As we *just* talked about literally a second ago. . ."

"Haha," said Pig Newton. "Got you!"

The Amazing Frog rolled his eyes. Pig Newton could be quite tricky when he wanted to. The Amazing Frog rode in silence the rest of the way to prevent further jokes at his expense. Pig Newton carried him up the steps of the police station. It was a large square building in the center of downtown Swindon. A frog police officer lingered on the steps outside. He looked very much like the Amazing Frog, except that he had a police hat, a badge, and some cool-looking mirrored sunglasses.

The Amazing Frog climbed down from Pig Newton's back. (Really, he threw himself off the pig's back until he landed in a pile of limbs on the ground, but that was how the Amazing Frog preferred to do things. Throwing yourself off of Pig Newton's back wasn't quite as fun as throwing yourself off a skyscraper, but you had to take what you could get.)

The Amazing Frog and Pig Newton walked up to the police officer frog.

"We need to file a missing pig report," said the Amazing Frog. "Pig Girl has gone missing."

"I see," said the police frog. "Have you tried. . . *looking right next to you*? Because there's a pig standing there."

"Don't be silly!" said the Amazing Frog. "That's Pig Newton. We are looking for a completely different pig."

"Oh," said the frog policeman. "Well, you never know. Sometimes the pig you're looking for is the one right in front of your face. You'd be surprised how frequently that happens. People come in looking for a certain pig, and they forget it's been following them the whole time."

"Can I speak to a supervisor of some sort. . .or just, you know, a smarter frog policeman?" the Amazing Frog asked testily.

"Sure," the police frog said. "The chief's inside behind the counter."

The Amazing Frog and Pig Newton walked past the officer, opened the door to the police station, and went inside. Sure enough, there was a long reception desk with a frog police chief standing just behind it. At one side of the room was a large jail cell. Inside was frog criminal. The Amazing Frog could tell this because he was wearing a mask and had black and white striped clothes on.

"Do they always dress like that?" the Amazing Frog asked the police chief.

"Dress like that?" said the chief. "How do you mean?"

"The criminals. . ." said the Amazing Frog. "They always wear masks and stripes. Doesn't that make it easier for you to see them? And catch them?"

"But they're criminals," said the chief. "That's how they're *supposed* to dress."

"Yeah," said another voice.

It was the criminal inside the cell. He had been eavesdropping through the bars.

"If you're asking about how criminals should dress, then it shows you really don't know the first thing about being one," the criminal added.

The chief nodded, apparently in agreement.

"He's right," said the chief. "Knowing how criminals should dress is just one reason that *I'm* the law-enforcement expert and *you're* not. No offense."

The Amazing Frog did not feel offended, just annoyed.

"That's good," said the Amazing Frog. "Because a law-enforcement expert is who we need to talk to. Pig Girl has gone missing. We don't know where she is."

"She didn't show up for breakfast!" added Pig Newton. "Breakfast is a big deal for pigs. It's the most important meal of the day. Also the most delicious. Pigs eat scraps, and when scraps sit overnight, they get all gooey and mushy. . .which makes them even more delicious than usual! Breakfast scraps are the best scraps! I don't know what could be important enough to make Pig Girl miss her breakfast scraps. I'm very worried about her."

"That *is* quite serious," said the chief. "And for a reason you might not know about. You see, there has been a rash of disappearances in Swindon recently."

"'Rash' is policeman-speak for 'a bunch of them,'" the Amazing Frog informed Pig Newton.

The pig nodded seriously.

"Yes," continued the chief. "A whole bunch of people have gone missing. My team of frog police is still analyzing the clues and trying to figure out who—or what—is behind it. Tell me, where was the last place you saw Pig Girl?"

Pig Newton thought for a moment.

"Two days ago I saw her playing underneath the willow trees on the hills to the west of Swindon," he said. "That's one of her favorite spots."

"We should go investigate the area," said the chief. "There might be some clues that would help us figure out what's going on. Plus, I bet we'll totally get to see where the best willow trees are. Pigs have a way of just knowing those things."

"Sounds good to me," said Pig Newton.

The three of them left the frog police station and set off toward the west side of Swindon. The streets were filled with interesting frogs running to and fro. The Amazing Frog wondered if any of them might have seen Pig Girl. He wanted to stop and question them all, but there were just too many! He tried to force himself to stay focused on their immediate objective. The Amazing Frog hoped that nothing serious had happened to Pig Girl. Maybe she had just gotten confused and wandered away. Pigs could be easily disoriented. It was one of their defining features. This was something that years of friendship with Pig Newton had taught the Amazing Frog. Pigs often never quite knew where they were going, even when they got there!

As they followed Pig Newton to the last place he'd seen pig girl, the Amazing Frog wondered if their piggy guide had any real idea where he was going.

As it turned out. . . he did.

They left the outskirts of Swindon and journeyed over a green, craggy landscape. The Amazing Frog seldom paid much attention to these sort of places. He thought of them as "flyover." Or maybe "cannon-over." These were places he normally flew across really quickly by shooting himself out of a cannon. Cannon was the only way to travel as far as the Amazing Frog was concerned. It was fun and exciting, and left you smelling of the pleasant aroma of burn gunpowder for the rest of the day.

Soon, in the distance ahead, the Amazing Frog spied what indeed appeared to be a grove of willow trees with a big pit of mud in front of it.

"There it is," said Pig Newton excitedly. "This is Pig Girl's favorite place. Nice cool mud, and trees to keep you shaded even when the sun is very hot."

"Let's look for clues," said the frog police chief. "The first thing I've learned about looking for clues is that it's bad to step on them. It usually destroys the clue. Or at least gets clue on the bottom of your shoe and then you have to scrape it off. Very inconvenient."

The Amazing Frog was starting to think maybe he would do a better job of finding Pig Girl than the frog police chief. The chief seemed a little bit silly and more than a little bit distracted. He was almost as bad as a pig on that account.

They reached the muddy pit underneath the willow trees and began to look around. The Amazing Frog didn't see anything unusual. . . at least not at first.

"Oh no," Pig Newton suddenly cried. "Something just went 'crunch' underneath my hoof. I'm afraid I've stepped on a clue."

"No," said the frog police chief confidently. "That's a leaf. One of the first things they teach you at the frog police academy is that a leaf is different from a clue."

"Oh, that's good to know," Pig Newton said with great relief. "Thank goodness we brought along a real professional. We're so lucky you're here. Isn't that right, Amazing Frog?"

The Amazing Frog was not so sure. He was looking carefully at the leaves underneath the willow trees, and how they had fallen into the mud.

"Chief," the Amazing Frog said. "I know you just said that leaves and clues are not the same thing, but have a look at these leaves over here in the mud pit."

The chief walked over and surveyed the scene.

"Yes," he said. "A whole lot of leaves that aren't clues is what you've got there. Typical. Leaves not being clues. I see it all the time."

"Uh-huh," said the Amazing Frog. "But don't you think it's interesting that these leaves have been arranged to spell out words. Almost like they were placed *intentionally* that way by someone."

"They have?" said the surprised police chief. "I mean. . . They have! They sure have. So. . . What exactly do they say?"

"Have a look for yourself," said the Amazing Frog.

All three of them looked at the leaves.

They spelled out: "WHEN IS A DOOR NOT A DOOR?"

For a moment, nobody said anything.

Then Pig Newton cried: "Oh, I know that one! When is a door not a door? When it's ajar! Like the word 'ajar,' but also it could mean a jar that you keep food inside of. That's why it's a joke. Words can be so confusing sometimes."

"A joke, eh?" said the frog police chief, rubbing his tiny chin thoughtfully. "Just as I feared."

"Just as you feared?" said the Amazing Frog. "You didn't say anything about fearing jokes! What is this 'fear' you're feeling?"

"It's the strangest thing," said the chief. "All around Swindon, people have been disappearing! Whenever we go and have a look at the last place they were seen, we always find a. . . joke."

"A joke?" said Pig Newton. "Well that's in poor taste. There's nothing funny about going missing. Because then people can't find you again. It's very inconvenient."

"Yes," agreed the chief. "The disappearances are a big problem. I'm beginning to think they're all connected. And the *real* problem is that the jokes aren't even that funny. I don't think I've laughed once!"

The Amazing Frog thought he might know what was going on.

"You said *jokes* were found at each scene?" said the Amazing Frog.

"Yes," said the chief.

"If it's not too much trouble, could you take me to some of these other jokes that were left behind?" asked the Amazing Frog.

"Um, I suppose so," said the chief. "But aren't we here to find Pig Girl?"

"Yes," said the Amazing Frog. "But I have this crazy idea that the more information we have, the better chance we're going to have of finding her. If the other people disappearing are connected to Pig Girl disappearing . . . then knowing *how* they're connected could really help us out!"

"Gee, when you put it that way, it makes a kind of sense," said the chief. "Okay. Let's go and look at some jokes."

They did.

The frog police chief took the Amazing Frog and Pig Newton all around Swindon and showed them places where different jokes had been left behind. Sometimes they were written on the ground or on the wall of a house. Other times things had been arranged to spell out jokes. But they were always very, very bad jokes. The Amazing Frog knew how important it was to pick up random trash, so he was a bit startled when they rounded a corner and found several pieces of trash strewn about in a very purposeful way.

"Why are fish so smart?" the Amazing Frog said, reading a pile of trash that had been shaped into letters. "Because they swim in schools."

"That's silly," opined Pig Newton. "Most of the fish I know aren't very smart at all."

"It's another joke," said the Amazing Frog. "There certainly *are* a lot of jokes being left behind."

"Yeah," said the chief. "We've really got our hands full."

"Have you considered asking Joke Frog if he knows anything about this?" said the Amazing Frog. "After all, if there's anybody who's known for making jokes *and* being a criminal, it's Joke Frog. In fact, I'd say he's kind of cornered the market when it comes to that."

"Joke Frog!" said the chief, suddenly very scared. "But he-he-he's not a *normal* criminal. He's more like a supervillain."

"Oh, come on," said the Amazing Frog. "He's not so bad. I've tangled with him a bunch of times. And I usually win."

"Oh oh oh," said Pig Newton, raising his hoof. "I have a question."

"Yes?" said the Amazing Frog.

"What does Joke Frog want with Pig Girl?" asked Pig Newton. "And. . . what does he want with any of the other law-abiding frog citizens that he made disappear?"

"That's a very good question," said the Amazing Frog. "I think it's time we went to find out!"

"This sounds like an exciting quest," said the chief. "Can I come?"

The Amazing Frog looked the chief over and tried to think of a nice way to tell him no. The Amazing Frog knew the chief's bumbling would just get in the way of things. Plus, the chief might see a criminal and just start uncontrollably chasing after it. That would not be helpful if you needed to do a thing like, say, sneak up on Joke Frog.

"Gee chief," said the Amazing Frog. "I think you're far too important to come with us."

"I am?" said the chief.

"Oh yes," said the Amazing Frog. "The citizens of Swindon need you. Without you here, they wouldn't know what to do."

"They wouldn't?" said the chief. "I mean. . . You're *right!* They wouldn't."

"Yes," said the Amazing Frog, sensing the chief had swallowed the bait. "You absolutely have to be here. You're essential. It should be up to less-important individuals—like me and Pig Newton—to take fun, adventurous risks while you sit in the frog police station."

"I guess so," said the chief. "It all makes sense to me when you explain it like that. So where will you find Joke Frog?"

"Leave that to me," said the Amazing Frog.

And off he went with Pig Newton trailing behind.

## Chapter Two

The Amazing Frog and Pig Newton crept over the greenish tan landscape. The city of Swindon was now far in the distance. They could no longer even see it on the horizon when they turned around. There was only the sound of the wind blowing.

And the water lapping.

"Say," said Pig Newton. "Do you hear water?"

"Not only do I hear it, I smell it," said the Amazing Frog. "When we walk over the next hill, we'll be able to see it too."

"Oh," said Pig Newton.

The pig scrunched up his face in dissatisfaction. He felt like the Amazing Frog was not quite telling him everything.

"Why?" said Pig Newton.

"Why *what*?" replied the Amazing Frog.

"Why do I hear water?" said the pig. "And also smell it? And also *OMIGOSH* we're near the bay, aren't we!?!? We're near Swindon-on-Sea!"

"Calm down," said the Amazing Frog.

"But the lake is full of dangerous sharks!" Pig Newton pointed out. "It's full of Megalodon, the biggest shark of all!"

"It's also where Joke Frog likes to hang out," said the Amazing Frog. "It's an exciting place!"

"But I'm scared!" said Pig Newton. "Joke Frog is dangerous enough. But sharks are super dangerous! Megalodon is a giant shark who could eat you in just one bite! And the smaller sharks could do the job in like three or four bites—which is still really bad."

"Relax," said the Amazing Frog. "I know what I'm doing. How many of those sharks have I turned into sushi over the years?"

"Well. . ." said Pig Newton hesitantly.

"Come on," said the Amazing Frog. "Give me an answer. How many?"

"Lots and lots of them."

"Lots and lots of them is right," said the Amazing Frog. "Don't worry. I know how to handle myself around sharks. Sure, going to the beach is always a little risky, but now and then you've got to take little risks to get what you want. Like bringing Pig Girl home safe and sound."

"That's right!" said Pig Newton, suddenly filled with bravery. "Pig Girl is the whole reason we're here. I've got to find her, whatever the danger!"

And with that, Pig Newton went sprinting ahead over the hill and toward the beach. It was all the Amazing Frog could do to keep up with him.

The beach was empty. There was no sign of Joke Frog. This fact was clear right away to the Amazing Frog because Joke Frog was easy to spot. He wore his face painted white, had bright red lipstick, and a purple suit with a green tie. He was hard to look at, but at the same hard to look away from. It was a real contradiction.

The Amazing Frog did, however, hear a weird clicking noise. He didn't know if Joke Frog made a clicking noise, but anything was possible. Soon, however, the Amazing Frog realized he was hearing Pig Newton's teeth chattering.

"Stop that," said the Amazing Frog. "I'm trying to think."

"But I can't!" said Pig Newton. "I'm trying to be brave, but I'm still scared."

Suddenly, there was a great rushing of water. The Amazing Frog turned to the sea and saw a single shark's fin cruising just above the waterline. It was moving toward them. It was very, very large.

"Now, I'm *really* scared!" cried Pig Newton.

But the Amazing Frog wasn't scared. He strolled confidently down to the edge of the water and waited. After a moment, the single fin drew up to the beach and an enormous shark began to emerge. It was, literally, the biggest shark in the universe. It was a big as a house. Its wet, grey sharkskin gleamed in the sun. It looked at the Amazing Frog and opened its mouth very wide. Each one of its perfectly triangular teeth was the size of a person.

"Hello, Megalodon," the Amazing Frog said nonchalantly. "You want to move a little to the left? You're blocking my sun."

The giant creature ignored this command.

"Hello*, Amazing Frog,*" the great beast said in a deep voice full of contempt. "Although, I don't know why I have to say that first part."

"What 'first part?'" said the Amazing Frog.

"The *'Amazing*' part," said Megalodon, with breath that reeked of smaller, deader fish. "I mean, I don't get to call myself Amazing Megalodon. Why should you get to be Amazing Frog?  I do amazing stuff too, you know. One time, I ate an entire boat *and* the guy who was jet-skiing behind it in a single gulp!  No other shark can do that. Only me. But you don't find me going around asking to be called *'Amazing*', do you?"

The Amazing Frog chose to ignore this. He thought Megalodon was probably just in a bad mood because the Amazing Frog foiled his evil plans so frequently. Megalodon and Joke Frog were the two closest things that the greater Swindon area had to supervillains. The Amazing Frog suspected Megalodon would be even more annoyed when he realized they weren't even here to see him.

As usual, the Amazing Frog was right.

"Megalodon, have you seen Joke Frog?" the Amazing Frog asked. "We're looking for him. It's about something very important."

"Huh?" said Megalodon. "Joke Frog? Why aren't you looking for me? *I'm important too, darn it*!"

"Look, have you seen him or not?" asked the Amazing Frog. "We really need to find him."

"Yeah," added Pig Newton between anxious, clicking teeth. "Pig Girl has gone missing. So have some other frogs from downtown Swindon. We're trying to figure out what's happening. We think Joke Frog might be involved."

Megalodon suddenly looked like he was thinking very hard. His eyes rolled to the upper-left corners of their giant sockets. His wide mouth closed slightly as—for a very brief moment—he might be thinking about something other than food.

"Ahh, yes," Megalodon finally pronounced. "Now that you mention it, I *do* recall Joke Frog saying something about luring lots of people to his new secret lair. Actually, 'lair' is probably the wrong word. He made it sound more like a fortress or a castle. Something really, *really* impressive. And full of all kinds of traps and tricks sure to foil anybody who came inside."

"A castle?" said the Amazing Frog.

"Oh yes," Megalodon said. "He'd been working on it in secret for a long time. All supervillains need to have cool lairs. He was hoping to make his the coolest. He was going to fill it full of silver trophies from all around Swindon, and other neat things."

"And you said he planned to lure people there?" said Pig Newton.

"Yes," said Megalodon. "Or maybe just run up to them and grab them. Whatever's easier. Joke Frog usually takes the path of least resistance."

"Do you think he would leave a written joke behind at the scene when he captured somebody?" the nervous pig pressed.

"You know, now that you mention it, that sounds *exactly* like what he'd do," said Megalodon.

Pig Newton looked over at the Amazing Frog.

"I think I know what happened," said Pig Newton. "Joke Frog kidnapped poor Pig Girl and took her to this castle. We need to go rescue her!"

The Amazing Frog was a bit less certain.

"Megalodon, Joke Frog really told you all of this?" asked the Amazing Frog.

The enormous shark nodded.

"And did Joke Frog say *where* this secret fortress-castle-lair might be?"

"M*aaaaaaaaybe*," Megalodon said evilly.

"Maybe?" said the Amazing Frog. "What does that mean?"

The shark smiled a wide, Cheshire grin.

"It means *maybe* I'll tell you where Joke Frog's castle is. . . if you do something for me," said the shark.

"What?" said the Amazing Frog.

"I want to ride on the blimp," said Megalodon.

It was the Amazing Frog's turn to open his mouth very wide. He was so surprised he couldn't help it!

The blimp that circled around the skies of Swindon was one of the city's most recognizable features. It was piloted by a friendly frog whose only quirk was that he didn't like to wear very many clothes—

just his underwear. The Amazing Frog thought that was pretty weird, but ultimately harmless. (Besides, who was going to see that you were only wearing underwear when you were way up high in a blimp all day.) Sometimes the Amazing Frog liked to ride in the blimp. But more often than not, he just rode on top of it so that he could fall down from it and land on a car and smash it super, *super* hard.

It was hard enough for a frog to get on the blimp. How on earth did Megalodon expect to do it.

"You can't be serious," the Amazing Frog finally said.

"I *am* serious," said Megalodon. "You better take me seriously too if you want me to tell you where Joke Frog's castle is."

"But. . . But. . ." the Amazing Frog sputtered. "Why do you even want to ride on the blimp in the first place?"

"Every day I watch the blimp go by and think about how fun it would be," said Megalodon. "*You* get to ride the blimp all the time. Why can't I?"

"But you're so big, you'll never fit inside the cockpit," said the Amazing Frog.

"He could fit on top of the blimp," Pig Newton pointed out. "*You* ride on top of the blimp all the time."

The Amazing Frog gave Pig Newton an annoyed glance out of the corner of his eye.

"Don't encourage him," the Amazing Frog whispered.

But it was too late. Megalodon had heard Pig Newton, and now the idea was in his brain.

"I could ride on the top of the blimp, yes!" said the giant shark excitedly. "I'm big, but I'll still fit. And then I can look down over the top of Swindon and see everything! It'll be so exciting."

The Amazing Frog sat down on the ground and tried to think. How was he going to do this? Normally, he'd never be bothered with crazy requests from Megalodon. (Normally, he'd just be figuring out new ways to turn him into sushi!) But the Amazing Frog knew he had to keep the big picture in mind. It would be easy to give up and just go home when faced with such a crazy request, but the Amazing Frog couldn't let down Pig Newton and Pig Girl. They were some of his best friends. Even if they *were* pigs.

"Okay," the Amazing Frog said, getting back to his feet. "I think I've got an idea. Megalodon and Pig Newton? You both wait here. I'll be right back. And Megalodon, no eating Pig Newton while I'm away."

"No problem," said the shark. "I'll only eat him when you're here."

The Amazing Frog gave Megalodon a look to say he was not amused.

"Just joking!" said the shark. "But seriously, I do like eating pigs."

The Amazing Frog realized this was as close as he was ever likely to get to a promise to behave from Megalodon. He turned around and headed back toward Swindon as fast as his tiny froggy legs would carry him. His destination was clear.

## Chapter Three

The Amazing Frog reached the edge of Swindon and headed for the nearest trampoline. There were trampolines all over Swindon. The Amazing Frog seldom stopped to consider why this was the case, but knew that someone very sensible and with great foresight had placed them there. They made it so easy to get around. Or, more accurately, to get up. Which was the Amazing Frog's goal at the moment.

Jumping on the nearest trampoline, the Amazing Frog propelled himself high into the air. As he flew skyward, he looked. . . not up, but down. He was looking for the next thing to propel himself off of. It might be another trampoline, but it also might be the roof of a car. Cars had very springy roofs. If you hit them just right, it was like jumping off of a trampoline. . . or maybe even better!

The Amazing Frog took his time jumping from trampoline to trampoline, and from car to car. When he wanted to get even greater height, he powered himself up by farting. For most people, farting was a bodily annoyance. Not for the Amazing Frog! For him, it was an invaluable tool for getting places. It just happened to involve bad-smelling gas coming out of his butt. The Amazing Frog used his farts to propel himself even higher into the atmosphere.

Soon, it happened. The blimp came into view.

The Amazing Frog jumped higher and higher, until his arcing flights took him near the blimp's cockpit. The frog pilot recognized the Amazing Frog and waved.

A few leaps later, the Amazing Frog found the perfect trajectory to carry himself into the blimp's cockpit. He landed in a heap.

"Oh! What's up, Amazing Frog?" asked the pilot.

"Oof, hello there," said the Amazing Frog, slowly disentangling his limbs and rising to his feet.

"You're looking well," the pilot said. "I mean, you're wearing far too many clothes for good taste, but still."

The blimp pilot, as usual, was in his underwear.

"I'm hardly wearing any clothes at all!" the Amazing Frog protested.

"It could still be less," the pilot pointed out.

"Anyhow, I need you to do me a favor," the Amazing Frog said. "Can you steer this blimp over to Swindon-on-Sea?"

"Of course I can," said the pilot. "I can steer it anywhere. Although I don't know why you'd want to go *there.* Downtown Swindon is the place to see. It's full of buildings and people and cool, interesting things. And they're *really* interesting when you see them from way up high in a blimp."

"We're on a special mission today," explained the Amazing Frog.

"A special mission!" said the pilot. "That sounds exciting."

"Yes," the Amazing Frog continued. "And for this mission, I need you to do some special maneuvers. When we reach Swindon-on-Sea, I need you to go as low over the water as you can—almost touching the water, actually."

"But if I touch the water the blimp might crash," said the pilot.

"Right, that's why I said *almost* touching," the Amazing Frog replied.

"Okay," said the pilot. "I'll do it. This is sure going to be an exciting change from my normal route! Of course, it might be even more exciting if we were wearing less clothes. . ."

"We are wearing precisely the right amount of clothes!" insisted the Amazing Frog. "Now drive the blimp."

"It was worth a shot," said the half-naked pilot, and turned his attention back to the control panel in front of him.

As the Amazing Frog watched out the window, the frog pilot steered the blimp away from Swindon. The buildings below them got smaller and smaller, and farther and farther away. Soon they were entirely lost in the distance. Then a band of sheer cobalt blue appeared on the horizon. The frog pilot steered straight for it. Soon, the sea began to come into view.

The Amazing Frog glanced down at the beach and saw a small pink shape beside a substantially larger blue-gray shape right at the edge of the water.

"Well at least Megalodon didn't eat Pig Newton," the Amazing Frog said to himself. "Or if he did, then he threw him back up in one piece."

"Okay, this is Swindon-on-Sea," said the frog pilot.

"Very good," said the Amazing Frog. "What I want you to do is take us very low over the water and make passes again and again along the beach."

"Okay," said the frog pilot. "Until when? Like, when do I stop?"

"Um. . ." the Amazing Frog said, trying to choose his words carefully. "Keep doing it until something. . . surprising happens. And when that thing happens, take the blimp very high."

"Something surprising?" said the frog pilot skeptically.

The Amazing Frog nodded.

"But how will I know it's the right surprising thing?" asked the pilot. "I'm surprised all the time. For example, I was very surprised a few minutes ago when you jumped into this cockpit."

"It will be *very* surprising," said the Amazing Frog. "Trust me."

"Oh, okay," said the frog pilot. "I'll be on the lookout."

And with that, the Amazing Frog threw himself out of the cockpit of the blimp. He tumbled crazily through the air—limbs trailing behind him—until he landed—splat!—right beside Pig Newton and Megalodon on the beach.

"That was fast!" said Pig Newton. "How did you get the blimp to come so quickly."

"I just asked the pilot nicely," the Amazing Frog said.

"That guy always creeps me out," Pig Newton confided. "He says I wear too many clothes. . . and I don't wear any clothes at all!"

"The blimp!" cried Megalodon. "Yes! This is going to be awesome."

Then a shadow seemed to fall across Megalodon's face. His toothy smile became a toothy frown. His expression showed disappointment.

"But how am I ever going to ride on it?" the giant fish asked. "It's way up there, and I'm way down here!"

"Don't worry," said the Amazing Frog. "I've got a plan. Take a look over there."

The Amazing Frog pointed to the center of the inlet. There was a dock, and several cool-looking watercraft to ride (they had powerful engines and could probably go really fast!)—but the Amazing Frog was pointing at none of these things. He was pointing at a ramp that had been erected for the purpose of letting the watercraft riders propel themselves up into the air.

"The pilot is going to take the blimp very low to the water," the Amazing Frog explained to Megalodon. "When he does, you need to swim through the water fast and go up the ramp. It will launch you into the air and onto the back of the blimp. Then you can ride it around."

"Hmm," said Megalodon. "That's crazy, and probably dangerous, but it just might work."

As they looked on, the frog pilot took the blimp on its descent near the waterline. It headed out to sea a bit, and then circled back, low and slow over the waves. It was *so* low that the Amazing Frog worried the waves from the sea might splash it and get the windshield foggy. The blimp didn't have windshield wipers, because it was accustomed to going above any rainclouds.

"Okay," said the Amazing Frog. "We're just about ready. Megalodon, prepare yourself. When I give the word, swim like crazy toward that jump ramp. Swim like you mean it. Like there's a tasty frog you want to eat at the top of the ramp. Give it all your gusto. Everything you've got."

Megalodon looked nervous and excited, and nodded quickly.

"Okay, here we go," the Amazing Frog said. "One. . . Two. . . *Three*!"

As the blimp drew nearer, Megalodon took off at top speed across the water. His giant fins thrashed back and forth. He kicked up foam and mist that splashed Pig Newton right in the face.

"Ick," said Pig Newton. "Even when he's swimming *away* from you, Megalodon manages to be a jerk!"

Megalodon reached the bottom of the ramp. At the same moment, the blimp passed low on the other side. The giant shark shot up the ramp, flew into the air, and went onto the back of the blimp.

For a moment, the Amazing Frog was afraid the giant shark would slip off of the top of the blimp. But even though Megalodon was very wet and slippery, he was also very heavy. When he landed on the blimp, the top of it smooshed-down like a flattened pillow. The blimp's engines strained under Megalodon's weight, but the giant shark did not fall off and the airship stayed aloft.

Through the windshield of the cockpit, the Amazing Frog saw that the frog pilot's eyes had gone wide. The pilot correctly surmised that this was the *very surprising thing* he had been awaiting. So he turned the blimp skyward and began to carry the great shark up high into the air.

The Amazing Frog smiled from ear to ear. His plan had worked!

Then a thought crossed his mind, and he cupped his hands to his mouth.

"Hey," the Amazing Frog shouted up at the blimp. "What about your side of the bargain, Megalodon? We got you your blimp ride! So tell us where we can find Joke Frog's castle!"

"Go north up the coast as far as you can!" shouted Megalodon. "You'll eventually see it."

"How will we know what the castle looks like?" asked Pig Newton.

"You'll know it when you see it. . ." answered Megalodon. Then the shark began to laugh. It was an evil laugh. He laughed and laughed, until the blimp took him away into the distance.

"I didn't like the way Megalodon was laughing like that," Pig Newton said. "It's like he knows something bad. Something that we don't know yet."

"Don't let Megalodon mess with your head," said the Amazing Frog. "I'm sure he's just being his typical rude self. A guy who'll try to eat you will also laugh at you. It comes with the territory, I think."

"I guess you're right," said Pig Newton. "Anyhow, we should make for the castle. I don't want to leave Pig Girl waiting."

"That sounds good to me," said the Amazing Frog, and together they turned and began heading up the rocky shoreline.

## Chapter Four

The Amazing Frog and Pig Newton walked for a long time. The terrain around them became barren and rocky. And also boring. So, so boring.

"I'm booored," whined Pig Newton. "There's nothing out here. At first, I was trying to remember why I never go this way. But then I remembered. It's because it's sooooooo boring."

"Well, sometimes you have to do boring things if they're important," observed the Amazing Frog.

"Yeah, I guess," said Pig Newton. "But still. So. Bored."

Suddenly, something on the horizon caught the Amazing Frog's attention, and he stopped right in his tracks. The stop was so abrupt that it caused him to fall down, but that was nothing new. The Amazing Frog fell down all the time, and was good at it. He quickly got back to his feet and continued to stare up the coastline.

"What?" said Pig Newton. "Did you trip?  Again?"

"Look at that," the Amazing Frog said, ignoring his friend's question.

He pointed to the distance where a single white tower seemed to jut into the sky.

"That's odd," said Pig Newton. "I sure never noticed that before. Maybe I was wrong about it being so boring up here. They've got a nice tall tower at least. Ooh, do you think that's Joke Frog's castle?"

"Yes," said the Amazing Frog cautiously. "But we'll need to get closer for me to be absolutely sure."

They crept forward up the rocky coast. As they did so, the tower ahead of them seemed to grow and grow. Then they began to detect another, much shorter tower beside the first one. Then, when they finally crested a hill close enough that they could see the ground beneath the towers, they realized that they were connected. They were all part of the same structure.

"Okay, now I'm sure it's Joke Frog's castle," said the Amazing Frog. "Because it's a building in the shape of a giant 'J' painted white just like Joke Frog's face."

Pig Newton nodded.

"Subtle," said the hog.

Pig Newton began heading closer, but the Amazing Frog stuck out an arm to stop him.

"What?" said Pig Newton. "We're so close. We can't stop now!"

"We *are* very close," agreed the Amazing Frog. "That's why I stopped you. Have you even thought about what we're going to do when we get there?"

"Yes, I have!" said Pig Newton with an enthusiastic nod. "We're going to get Pig Girl back from Joke Frog!"

"Okay," said the Amazing Frog. "And what if he doesn't open the door and let you inside?"

"Then. . . Well, if. . ." sputtered Pig Newton. "Actually, I hadn't considered it. What *should* we do if he doesn't let us inside?"

"Don't worry," said the Amazing Frog confidently. "We're not even going to knock on the door. I've already thought of something else."

"Oh, good," said Pig Newton. "Because I didn't have any other ideas."

They moved closer to the tall, J-shaped castle that sat beside the sea. The Amazing Frog did not head directly for the front of the castle, but rather for the side of the building. Pig Newton followed curiously, wondering just what his friend might be up to. There was nobody about. No castle guards. No Pig Girl. And certainly no Joke Frog.

When they reached the foot of the tallest tower, the Amazing Frog paused and pointed up to the top of it, now nearly lost in the clouds.

"I *thought* so," he said proudly.

"Thought what?" said Pig Newton. "I still don't understand what your plan is."

"Do you see that tiny window at the top of the tower?" asked the Amazing Frog.

Pig Newton craned his neck skyward. If he squinted really, really hard, he thought just maybe he did see a small circular window.

"Somebody's left it open," said the Amazing Frog. "I'm going to climb up the side of this tower and go in through that window. Then we won't have to worry about tricking Joke Frog into opening the door, because I'll already be inside."

"It looks awfully high," said Pig Newton. "I'm glad you like heights, because I don't."

"What, are you scared?" the Amazing Frog asked, ribbing his friend in a good-natured way.

"No," said Pig Newton. "It's just harder to see grass, and truffles, and mud—all the things I like, basically—when you're way up high. All the good stuff is down on the ground. If there was a bunch of fun mud to play in way up in the sky, I'd be the first one there. But there isn't. So I'm not."

"Fair enough," said the Amazing Frog with a grin.

The Amazing Frog stepped back from the tower and prepared for his climb. A more careful person would have taken this time to gauge the angle of the tower, account for wind direction, and other science things. Not the Amazing Frog. He operated by launching himself at, into, or over stuff and hoping for the best. It was an approach that almost always worked for him. And if it didn't work, then at least something fun happened.

Even going by only his gut, the Amazing Frog knew it was going to take some quickness to get to the top of the tower. For this reason, he reached into his pocket and took out his emergency can of Croak Zero. Then he took a few steps back from the tower and began to drink it down.

"What's that?" asked Pig Newton.

"It's a Croak Zero," the Amazing Frog said between sips. "It gives me the vital nutrients I need to run really fast. The problem is, it also makes me talkreallyfast. OhnoIt'shappening. HereIgo!!!"

And with all his words slurring into one, the Amazing Frog sprinted toward the foot of the tower. He moved two or three times faster than he usually did, and he *already* moved pretty quickly. To Pig Newton, it looked like a froggy blur speeding past.

The Amazing Frog reached the the tower and propelled himself up the side of it. Luckily for him, the tower was not perfectly straight or smooth, but had many imperfections that let him get his webbed feet stuck in them for traction. It ended up being more like climbing a ladder than climbing a wall. The poor construction of the tower also caused pieces of it to flake off and fall to the ground as the Amazing Frog climbed higher and higher. He left a trail of white dust falling behind him. This gave him the appearance of a rocket taking off.

He was also like a rocket in that when he reached the top of the tower—and the circular window through which he might enter—the Amazing Frog did not immediately stop. Instead, his momentum carried him up into the air above. His limbs flailed around wildly.

"Oh, darn," said the Amazing Frog. "I always forget that this happens when I drink too much Croak Zero."

The Amazing Frog flew into the air above the tower. After a few moments, his velocity stopped carrying him upwards, and he started heading back down. There was just an instant in which his trajectory reversed itself. In that instant, the Amazing Frog tried to figure out what to do. The only solution seemed to be to hit the open window at a downward angle. In the split-second that passed, the Amazing Frog couldn't think of anything better, so he used his webbed feet like sails to guide his downward path in the direction of the window. Try as he might to angle himself properly, the Amazing Frog quickly realized he was still going to be a couple of feet short of his target. But he couldn't give up! The Amazing Frog called up all of his reserves. Which, in this case, were located in his butt.

The Amazing Frog farted as powerfully as he could. It was one of his all-time finest farts. A deep, soul-fart. It made a noise like a cannon as it came out of his backside. The sound boomed across the landscape and echoed off the distant hills.

From far down below him, in the deafening silence that followed the flatulence, the Amazing Frog heard Pig Newton exclaim: "Wow!"

More importantly than its making an impressive sound, the Amazing Frog's gas adjusted the direction of his fall and blew him into the open window of Joke Frog's castle. The Amazing Frog landed in a heap on a stone floor. The room around him was barren and empty. A single staircase in the middle of the floor led down to unseen depths.

The Amazing Frog gathered himself and crept over to the window. He looked through it and down to the ground below. He waved at Pig Newton.

"That was *some* leap!" sand Pig Newton. "And *some* fart!"

"Thank you," said the Amazing Frog. "I'll try to open the front door from the inside if I can. But I don't know what I'm going to to find inside here, or how long it will take me. Wish me luck!"

"Good luck!" called Pig Newton.

The Amazing Frog turned his attention back to the inside of the tower. He crept over to the staircase leading down below into the darkness. He did not know what he would find—or what devious traps or tricks Joke Frog might have in store for him—but knew he would have to be careful. Yet he did not hesitate to make his way down the scary dark staircase. (A lesser frog might have been afraid to proceed, but *not* the Amazing Frog. He was totally brave!)

The Amazing Frog made his way down the staircase. It looped in a spiral as it went down. It took a long time for the Amazing Frog to walk down all of the steps. The Amazing Frog was a guy who liked action. Descending a winding staircase made him a little impatient. He thought about simply flinging himself down the steps, but he knew that this approach might mean flinging himself into one of Joke Frog's traps. He decided to be careful instead.

After what seemed like a very, very long time, the Amazing Frog reached the bottom of the staircase. There, he saw a strange sight!  At the foot of the stair was a large chamber with a very high ceiling. Inside the chamber was an enormous cage—like a birdcage, but huge. Inside the enormous cage were several frogs. One of them wore white paint and red lipstick on his face, had a purple suit, and around his neck was a neon-green necktie.

The Amazing Frog was stunned. He couldn't understand why Joke Frog would be in a cage inside his own castle. Or why other frogs would be trapped in there with him.

Then something more surprising happened! Some of the frogs walked to a different part of the cage, and behind where they had been standing was a round pink blob. The light was still quite dim, but even in the reduced visibility, the Amazing Frog could see that the pink blob was familiar to him.

"Pig Girl!" exclaimed the Amazing Frog.

He rushed over to the cage.

"Ooh, look," said one of the frogs inside. "It's the Amazing Frog. He's come to rescue us. I *knew* someone would!"

"Yay!" cried another. "It was so boring in here. I mean, Joke Frog killed some time for us by telling jokes, but they weren't good jokes. They were bad. Maybe they should call him Bad Joke Frog."

"I don't care what we call him," said a third frog. "Just so long as we don't have to listen to him anymore! I'm so glad we finally had the sense to tie his mouth shut."

Now that the Amazing Frog looked closer, he saw that a napkin had been tied around Joke Frog's mouth. That was probably the only reason he wasn't telling more jokes at that very moment.

The Amazing Frog reached the cage. He ignored the other frogs—and even Joke Frog—and kept his attention on Pig Girl.

"Pig Girl," said the Amazing Frog. "Are you okay? How did you get trapped in that cage? Did Joke Frog do this to you?"

"Actually, I don't think he did," Pig Girl said, sounding quite confused.

"Tell me what happened," said the Amazing Frog. "While you do that, I'll try to figure a way to get you out of this cage!"

"Well, I was heading for my favorite spot of willow trees—like I do almost every day—but when I got there, a strange surprise was waiting for me," explained Pig Girl. "It was a note. Someone had left it on the ground, right in the middle of a mud puddle. I cleaned off the mud, and saw that it had my name on it! It was a note *for me."*

"What did it say?" asked the Amazing Frog.

"The note said I had won a special prize. It said that to claim the prize, all I had to do was to come to this castle. On the back of the note was a map showing how to get there. The note said that in return for the prize, I only needed to do two things. One, I needed to keep it a secret and not tell anybody where I was going. And two, it said that before I left for the castle, I should leave behind a. . . joke."

"A joke?" said the Amazing Frog.

Pig Girl nodded.

"Specifically, a bad joke," she explained. "I didn't have anything to write with, so I left behind my joke using leaves that had fallen off the trees. Then I headed to where the map said to go, hoping to claim my prize."

"That's what happened to the rest of us, too!" one of the other frogs in the cage suddenly chimed-in. "All of us found notes saying that we should secretly come to this castle, and that we should leave behind some kind of joke before we left."

"That is very odd," said the Amazing Frog.

"It got even odder once we arrived at the castle," said Pig Girl. "I knocked on the door with my hoof and said that I was here to claim my prize. Then the door opened, but it was very dark inside and I couldn't see anything. Suddenly, someone grabbed me and pulled me into the darkness. I couldn't tell what was happening. Then, when my eyes began to adjust to the gloom, I was already trapped inside this big cage."

"Did Joke Frog grab you and throw you in the cage?" asked the Amazing Frog.

"No," said Pig Girl. "It was dark and I couldn't see much, but whoever grabbed me was wet and slippery. And smelled like salt water."

"Wet and smelled like salt water. . ." the Amazing Frog said, considering this clue very carefully. "That only describes Joke Frog *some* of the time. Like right after he's been swimming."

The Amazing Frog walked along the side of the cage until he reached the spot where Joke Frog was sitting. The comedian looked unusually grumpy. But—reasoned the Amazing Frog—that might have only been because somebody had tied his mouth shut.

"Can you guys take that thing out of his mouth?" said the Amazing Frog. "I need to talk to him."

"If you say so," one of the frogs replied. "But I warn you, he's probably just going to start telling jokes again."

"That's okay," said the Amazing Frog. "I've been around Joke Frog before. I'm used to it."

The other frogs inside the giant cage took the napkin off of Joke Frog's mouth.

"Now," began the Amazing Frog, "something very serious has happened here, Joke Frog. I'm not exactly sure how you're involved, but I-"

"What do you call a belt made out of watches?" Joke Frog nearly shouted, cutting him off.

"Joke Frog, be serious for once, and don't interrupt-"

"A *waist* of time!" exclaimed Joke Frog. "Get it? 'Waist' like where your belt goes? Ehh?"

"I got it," said the Amazing Frog. "It's horrible, but I got it."

"See," one of the other frogs inside the cage said. "What did we tell you? He's always like this. It's why we had to put a napkin over his mouth."

"Joke Frog, did you lure all these people here and trap them?" the Amazing Frog asked. "That's a very impolite thing to do. People have busy schedules. They can't spend all day being trapped in a cage with you. . . even if it *is* the only way you'll ever get yourself a captive audience."

Joke Frog looked around the cage. Then he frowned, which was rare to see him do. Then he leaned in very close and whispered so that only the Amazing Frog could hear him.

"Don't make me break character," pled Joke Frog. "Please. I've got a reputation to keep up. People need to know that I'm a hilarious comedian all the time."

The Amazing Frog smacked his own forehead in frustration.

"Okay," he said, "first of all? You're not a hilarious comedian. You're a *terrible* comedian. Second of all, you have to break character when serious things happen. And this is serious."

"But. . . But. . ." Joke Frog protested.

"Look," said the Amazing Frog, getting even more annoyed. "This can go two ways. You can help me and maybe I let you out of the cage, or you can be a jerk. If you choose to be a jerk, I'll leave you in the cage with a napkin over your mouth, and you won't be able to tell any jokes at all. It's your choice."

"Okay, *fine*," said Joke Frog, hanging his head in defeat. "No more jokes. For now."

"Good," said the Amazing Frog. "Now tell me what happened."

"I'm as confused as anyone else!" Joke Frog explained. "This isn't even my castle."

"It isn't?" said the Amazing Frog. "Because it's shaped like a giant J for Joke Frog."

"But it's not my castle!" Joke Frog repeated. "I don't even *have* a castle. I have a hideout. Real supervillains have hideouts. Not castle or lairs or whatever. It's totally different. I could take you to my hideout and show you to prove it . . .if I ever got out of here."

"Then how did you get trapped inside this giant cage with these people?" the Amazing Frog asked suspiciously.

"Believe it or not, I received a mysterious note, just like everyone else here," said Joke Frog. "It was waiting for me on the door of my hideout. But mine didn't say to leave behind a joke to get a special prize. Instead, it said that someone had built a castle for me, and all I had to do was show up to claim it. Free castle.

No strings attached. I was too excited to be suspicious. I followed where the map said to go, and ended up here at this castle. I knocked on the door and went inside. Then, somebody who smelled like saltwater grabbed me and threw me in this cage. It was so dark I never saw them."

It was a very strange tale that Joke Frog was telling, but the Amazing Frog believed it. Joke Frog was known for telling horrible jokes and being a jerk, but not for lying. The Amazing Frog thought the villain was shooting straight with him for once.

"Hmm," said the Amazing Frog. "Okay. I need to think about this and figure out what's going on. I also need to figure out how to get you all out of this giant cage. While I do that, I'm going to let Pig Newton inside."

"Oh!" said Pig Girl, her face lighting up. "Pig Newton is here? He's so handsome and brave. I mean, you know. . .for a pig."

The Amazing Frog smiled and headed for the front door of the castle. The door was barred with a large beam of wood, but he easily removed it. Then, as he prepared to open the door, he noticed something strange. Placed directly on either side of the door were stone pools. These pools were filled with salt water.

"Very, very strange," the Amazing Frog said to himself.

Then he threw open the door and daylight streamed inside. The daylight was shortly followed by a very excited pig.

"Omigosh!" shouted Pig Newton, nearly knocking the Amazing Frog over with his enthusiasm. "You did it! You opened the door. Oh, and you found Pig Girl too! Why, this is wonderful. But she's trapped in a cage with a bunch of frogs!"

"Don't worry," said the Amazing Frog. "We're going to get her out of there. Or, more precisely, *you* are?"

"I am?" said Pig Newton.

"My hero!" Pig Girl swooned from inside the cage.

"I am?. . . I mean. . . *I AM*!" Pig Newton said confidently.

The Amazing Frog turned Pig Newton's attention to the top of the cage, so high up that it was nearly lost in the darkness.

"See that?" the Amazing Frog said, extending a finger. "At the top of the cage is a chain. I'm guessing that whoever trapped everybody here was using the chain to raise and lower the cage."

"Hmm," said Pig Newton. "That makes sense."

"Yes," said the Amazing Frog, "and if you look closely, you can see the chain loops around the top of the room, and eventually goes down the side of the wall, until it ends. . . right here."

The Amazing Frog pointed to a length of chain along the wall just beside Pig Newton, near one of the watery pools. It terminated in a kind of bridle or harness, like a horse might use. Pig Newton eyed the strange equipment warily.

"What's that?" the pig asked.

"I think it's a harness that somebody used to lower the cage when people came into the castle," the Amazing Frog said. "I also think we can use it to raise the cage and get everyone out."

Pig Newton investigated the harness. He seemed skeptical.

"It's pretty big," said the pig.

"Yes," said the Amazing Frog. "It's far too big to fit around me. I think it's meant for something wider. Like, for example, a *shark*."

"A shark?" said Pig Newton.

The Amazing Frog nodded.

"But I also think it just might fit around a pig who was the right size. Your size, for example."

Gulp. Pig Newton swallowed hard.

"Come on," said the Amazing Frog. "You can totally do this. Everybody's depending on you, and that includes your girlfriend over."

"I guess so," said Pig Newton, strapping himself into the harness. "What am I supposed to do . . . now that this thing is on me?"

"Try walking toward the door of the castle," the Amazing Frog suggested. "When you pull on the chain, it will lift the cage. The further you can pull it, the higher the cage will go."

"Oh," said Pig Newton. "That's not very complicated at all, is it? I thought there was going to be some kind of trick to it."

"No trick," said the Amazing Frog.

The pig made a break for the castle door, pulling hard on the chain.

"Hnnng, unnng, uurrrrgh!" said Pig Newton, making hard pulling noises.

The chain moved a few inches. On the other side of the cavernous room, the giant cage lifted a couple of inches off the ground.

"It's not high enough!" shouted the frogs. "You'll have to do better than that."

Suddenly, the strain became too much for Pig Newton. He stopped pulling and the harness jolted him back to his original position. The enormous cage clunked back down against the cavern floor.

Pig Newton chuffed in frustration.

"I. . . I. . . almost did it," the pig said. "I just need a little more of. . . What do you call it again when you're riding on my back and I go too slow, so you shout things at me to make me go faster? Motor-vation?"

The Amazing Frog laughed.

"Motivation," he said to Pig Newton. "That's what you're thinking of."

"Oh yeah," said the pig. "I need some more of that. Why don't you get on my back?"

The Amazing Frog squinted, as though he hadn't heard Pig Newton correctly.

"But Pig Newton, if I ride on your back, you'll have to carry me *in addition* to lifting the cage. It'll make it much harder for you."

"That's okay," said Pig Newton. "You'll make up for it with the motor-vation."

"Motivation," said the Amazing Frog.

"Whatever, just get on," said the pig.

The Amazing Frog climbed onto Pig Newton's back, being very careful not to get tangled in the harness.

"Okay," said Pig Newton. "Now motor-vate me!"

The Amazing Frog rolled his eyes. Then he did his best to motivate his friend.

"Okay Pig Newton," the Amazing Frog began. "I want you to start pulling. Pull as hard as you can, and don't stop pulling. Pull!!!"

The pig strained hard and the cage began to lift off of the castle floor.

"Yes, that's good," said the Amazing Frog. "Keep going. Think about all the poor frogs inside of the cage who you want to save. They got lured here by some kind of dirty trick, and didn't deserve to be trapped in a cage. And think about Joke Frog. His jokes aren't funny, but he didn't deserve to be trapped in the cage either. And then think about your girlfriend, Pig Girl. Just think how proud of you she's going to be when you free her from the cage. I bet she gives you a big muddy kiss, right on the end of your pig snout. I bet she-"

A voice interrupted the Amazing Frog.

"Okay, you can stop now," it said. "The cage is like ten feet off the ground."

The Amazing Frog swiveled his head around. Sure enough, he had motivated Pig Newton so much that the tough little pig had moved the harness several feet across the floor. The cage was dangling high in the air and all the frogs—and Pig Girl too—had escaped.

"Yay!" called Pig Newton. "We did it!"

Pig Newton relaxed. The moment he did, the heavy cage clattered back to the castle's stone floor with a THUD. The harness jerked back ten feet in less than a second. The Amazing Frog went flying off of Pig Newton's back and careening across the room. He landed on the floor in a familiar heap.

"Oh," said Pig Newton, climbing out of the harness. "Sorry about that."

Pig Girl ran up to Pig Newton and gave him a kiss on the snout. Pig Newton blushed and turned red. The Amazing Frog disentangled himself and stood up. Then he walked back across the floor to where everyone had gathered.

"Thank you for freeing us!" the frogs exclaimed. "We'll tell everyone back in Swindon about the brave thing you did. You might even get some sort of reward."

"That sounds nice," said Pig Newton.

"Yes," said another of the frogs. "You might even get knighted by the Frog King."

"Really?" said Pig Newton, now feeling very full of himself. "Being a knight sounds awfully glamorous. Do you suppose I can get a suit of armor made for a pig?"

"I hate to be a buzzkill, but I don't know if the Frog King can make you a real knight," said the Amazing Frog. "Because I don't think he's a real king. He's more like a guy who just hangs out downtown all day and wears a crown."

"Oh," said Pig Newton. "Well I still might get a suit of armor . . . just for fun."

"You would look totally dashing in a suit of armor!" agreed Pig Girl, and kissed him on the snout again.

The Amazing Frog cleared his throat.

"I don't think it's time to start celebrating and armor-shopping quite yet," he said seriously. "We still need to figure out exactly what happened here, and why all of you were lured to this castle. And unfortunately, I think I might have just done it."

"Oh," said Pig Newton in surprise. "When did you figure it out?"

"When I was flying across the room just now," said the Amazing Frog. "I do all of my best thinking when I'm flying through the air."

"What did you figure out when you were flying through the air?" asked Joke Frog. "And it better not be that this was my fault, because it isn't. I didn't do any of this, and that's the truth!"

"For once, I agree with you," said the Amazing Frog. "You are innocent, Joke Frog."

"He is?" said one of the frogs. "Then who was it?"

"Think about it," urged the Amazing Frog. "Whoever did this clearly wanted everyone to *think* that Joke Frog was behind the plot. Leaving bad jokes at the scene of the disappearances—building a big castle in the shape of a J—these are all things meant to make the authorities believe that Joke Frog was behind it all."

"Wow, I've been framed," said Joke Frog. "So *this* is what it feels like. Usually it's me framing other people!"

"But wait, why would you want to frame Joke Frog?" asked Pig Newton. "He's *already* a villain. That would be like someone starting a rumor that *you* could jump really high and fart powerfully. They wouldn't accomplish anything by that. Everyone already knows that's true."

"I think what they wanted was to get us to come here to this castle, to try to rescue everyone," the Amazing Frog said.

"What good would that do?" Pig Newton said dismissively. "So we rescued these folks. All we had to do was lift up the cage. It wasn't even that hard, at least not when I had the proper motor-vation."

Pig Girl kissed Pig Newton again, to show she was still proud of her hero.

"What that does is get us out of Swindon for a while," the Amazing Frog said with grave concern. "More precisely, it leaves Swindon *undefended*."

"Undefended?" said Pig Newton. "But who would want to. . ."

But Pig Newton trailed off. The answer had already occurred to him.

"Megalodon and the sharks!" cried Pig Newton.

"I'm afraid so," said the Amazing Frog. "I think they had this castle built, and I think they sent those letters to everyone. And I think two sharks waited here in the darkness in these water pools by the door, and threw everyone into the cage, one-by-one, as they arrived. They did all of this because they knew it would distract us. . . from what I'm starting to think must be something very nasty they want to do in downtown Swindon."

"But how would sharks even get to Swindon, and what would they do when they got there?" asked Pig Newton.

"That's what we've got to find out!" explained the Amazing Frog. "It could involve shark frogs. It could involve them invading the swimming pools of Swindon. Megalodon has made his way downtown before. Sure, he just flopped around and crushed people, but maybe since then he's thought about a better approach. And I'll tell you one thing. Whatever it is, it isn't good for us."

"It sounds like we need to get back to Swindon as quickly as possible and put a stop to whatever Megalodon might have in mind," said Pig Newton.

"I agree," said the Amazing Frog. "I just wish we hadn't given him a blimp ride to exactly where he wanted to go."

"Oh," said Pig Newton brightly, remembering. "We *did* do that, didn't we? Or, really, *you* did. It was *you* who set that up."

"Thanks for reminding me," the Amazing Frog said sarcastically. "Now let's not waste any more time. We need to get back to Swindon to save it...before its too late!"

## Chapter Five

Swindon slowly came into view in the distance. The tall towers first, then the smaller buildings, and then finally the streets and cars and businesses. The Amazing Frog huddled on the side of a hill and looked down into Swindon with a careful eye. Behind him, Pig Newton, Pig Girl, Joke Frog, and the group of recently-freed frogs all did the same.

As they looked, they all had the same question.

"Where is everybody?" asked Pig Newton.

"Yeah," added Pig Girl. "I was expecting to see frogs. And if the sharks had invaded, I was expecting to see a bunch of shark fins moving around and peeking over the tops of the houses. But I don't really see anything. It's just. . . empty, isn't it?"

"First looks can be deceiving," said the Amazing Frog. "But you're definitely correct about one thing. There's nobody on the streets today."

"Ooh," said Pig Newton. "What if it's some sort of frog holiday?"

"Frog holiday?" asked Pig Girl.

"Yeah, said Pig Newton. "I can never remember them all—probably because I'm a pig, not a frog—but there are always special days when the banks and stores are closed, and I wonder why, and then I find out it's a frog holiday."

"Nope, it's not a holiday today," said one of the frogs in the group behind them.

"That's right," said another frog. "I think the next holiday is Frogsmas. It's not for another three weeks. Oh, how I like Frogsmas!  Such a fun holiday. So many presents!  In my book, it's right up there with Frog's Year Day and the Frog Festival."

The Amazing Frog turned to face the group.

"We're going to have to go investigate," he said. "It's the only way we can learn more. Pig Newton, I want you to come with me."

"Absolutely," said the pig.

"And Joke Frog. . . I want you to come too!"

"What? *Me*?" said Joke Frog.

"Yes, you," the Amazing Frog insisted. "I have a feeling that you're going to be important to solving this, one way or another."

"Oh," said Joke Frog. "Okay. But I might tell some jokes along the way."

"We'll have to take you any way we can get you," the Amazing Frog said with a shrug.

And with that, the three of them crept into the outskirts of Swindon.

"It's so empty," whispered Pig Newton. "It's like a ghost town. Or, ooh, what if zombies drove everyone away. Maybe it's a zombie town!"

"Have you seen Zombie Pig Newton recently?" asked the Amazing Frog, referring to Pig Newton's undead alter ego. "Maybe he would know."

"Nah," said Pig Newton. "I haven't seen him in a while. If we pass any pig cemeteries or graveyards along the way, we might run into him though. He's a pretty friendly guy. When he's not trying to eat your brain, that is."

"I think that's true of most zombies," said the Amazing Frog with a grin. "They can be quite charming . . . until the brain-eating part comes up."

"What do vegan zombies eat?" asked Joke Frog.

The Amazing Frog and Pig Newton looked at him.

"Graaaaaaaaains," said Joke Frog.

The Amazing Frog shook his head.

"You know zombie jokes too? Is there any subject you *can't* joke about?"

"I haven't been stumped yet," Joke Frog said proudly. "But there could always be a first time."

They carried on deeper into Swindon. The buildings began to rise high around them, but there was still no sign of any of the residents. It was eerily quiet—which, according to the Amazing Frog, was the worst kind of quiet there was.

"Maybe everybody's inside," said Pig Newton. "Like it's one of those days when there's really bad smog or air pollution, or there's a lot of pollen in the air from flowers. Something like that. What do you think?"

"Honestly, I think probably not," said the Amazing Frog. "But there's one way to check."

The Amazing Frog walked up to the nearest building and threw open the door. It was a Frog Milk Coffee café. The familiar green and white logo would have been welcoming under other circumstances, or at least made the Amazing Frog think about how he was about to enjoy a delicious drink. But that was not the case today. The entire place was empty. No frog customers. No frog employees.

Pig Newton walked into the café.

"Well," he said, "at least there are a lot of Croak Zeros you could take for free."

"Pig Newton, that's stealing," said the Amazing Frog. "Though you *could* probably get away with it, because I haven't seen any frog police officers either. This is *very* strange."

They went back outside and continued their journey around downtown Swindon.

"I've got an idea of where we might be able to find someone who can tell us what's going on," said the Amazing Frog.

"You do?" said Pig Newton.

The Amazing Frog gestured to the police station.

"Ahh, of course, the frog police chief," said the pig.

"No," said the Amazing Frog. "He's kind of inept. Whatever happened here, I expect he was the first person to hightail it for the hills. . .or wherever everybody went. My hope is that he's *so* inept that he forgot about the prisoners still in his jail."

The Amazing Frog opened up the door to the police station and strode inside. Pig Newton and Joke Frog followed. It was dim and empty. The usual bustle of frog police officers processing suspects and doing police work was entirely absent.

But the station was not empty!

Just as the Amazing Frog had forecasted, the barred door of the jail cell was still locked. Inside the cell was a frog criminal, with a mask over his eyes and striped clothes on his back. The frog criminal was looking out the tiny, barred window of the jail cell. He wore an expression like a dog that can see and smell a Christmas ham, but can't quite reach it.

"I gotta get out! I gotta get out! I gotta get out!" the frog criminal was chanting to himself.

"You!" said the Amazing Frog.

The criminal jumped so high on his froggy legs that he banged his head against the ceiling.

"Ouch," said the criminal. "Who are you guys? Never mind. It doesn't matter who you are. You *gotta* let me out! Please!"

"Why should we let you out?" asked the Amazing Frog suspiciously.

"Because the city's empty, and I could get away with *so many* crimes right now!" the criminal exclaimed. "All the frog police are gone. All the businesses have been left open. All the people are gone from their homes. I could just walk in and take whatever I wanted. *If I could only get out of this cell!*"

"Wait, what happened here?" asked the Amazing Frog. "Why is Swindon so empty?"

"It was the shark!" the criminal said. "And normally—being a criminal—I have a lot of respect for sharks. They do things any criminal could appreciate—like scaring people and not obeying any laws! But this time they went *too far*, even for sharks! It all started when Megalodon suddenly fell from the sky. I think he had ridden here on top of the blimp."

The Amazing Frog and Pig Newton exchanged a glance. The Amazing Frog kicked himself for ever having made an arrangement with a jerk like Megalodon.

"Then what happened?" the Amazing Frog pressed.

"All these other sharks showed up too," said the criminal. "There were lots and lots of them. They jumped into the swimming pools. They rode watercraft down the middle of the streets. They seemed to appear from out of nowhere. I'd never seen anything like it."

"But if a bunch of sharks took over the town, then how come we haven't seen one shark yet?" asked Pig Newton.

"They didn't stay," explained the frog criminal. "I don't think taking over Swindon was their plan. They chased everybody out of the city. They said all the frogs would head over to Swindon-on-Sea if they knew what was good for them."

"How would going to Swindon-on-Sea be good for them?" asked Pig Newton. "Frogs don't live in the water. Or wait, maybe that's toads. I have so much trouble keeping frogs and toads straight."

"I don't know why the sharks did it," the criminal continued. "But everybody followed their orders. All the frogs left Swindon for Swindon-on-Sea—even the police! Which was great for me, except they forgot that I was locked here in this jail cell. Now. . . *please let me out!"*

The Amazing Frog carefully considered the situation.

"First of all we're not going to let you out of the jail, because you're a frog criminal and you'll go around taking things that don't belong to you," the Amazing Frog said.

"Darn it!" said the frog criminal. "Well, it was worth a shot to ask. . ."

"Second of all, I think we need to get to Swindon-on-Sea and find out what those sharks are up to," said the Amazing Frog. "They've done some pretty rotten things before to the citizens of Swindon—but I'm starting to think this might be the rottenest thing ever."

"But what about me?" asked the criminal.

"Sorry," said the Amazing Frog. "You'll have to wait here until the frog police come back."

"Darn it again!" said the frog criminal. "I guess I'll keep looking out of this window looking at all the things I *could* be stealing. . .if I could just get out of here."

The Amazing Frog turned and prepared to leave the frog police station.

"Why do you think the sharks did this?" asked Pig Newton. "What do the sharks *want*?"

"I'm not sure yet," said the Amazing Frog. "But I think we'll know that very soon."

## Chapter Six

The Amazing Frog headed for Swindon-on-Sea. Pig Newton and Joke Frog followed him. None of them knew what they would find when they got there, but they were all curious to learn what was happening.

"Maybe it's something good!" conjectured Pig Newton.

"Good?" said the Amazing Frog.

"Yeah," Pig Newton said. "Like maybe they brought everybody to Swindon-on-Sea to give them a present. Like a new bouncy castle or something."

"Have you *ever* known the sharks to do something nice?" asked the Amazing Frog skeptically.

"Well, no," Pig Newton admitted. "But there's a first time for everything."

The Amazing Frog rolled his eyes.

"Or maybe this is some sort of joke the sharks are playing," Pig Newton said. "Like, we'll get there and they'll be like 'Haha, joke's on you!'"

"I don't think so," Joke Frog chimed in. "I'm an expert on jokes. If this is a joke, it's not a very good one."

The trio headed across the landscape in the direction of Swindon-on-Sea. Along the way, they encountered cast off bit of clothing. At one point, they found a police frog's mirror shades just sitting in the middle of the grass.

"Gee," said Pig Newton. "It looks like everybody *did* go this way."

"Yeah," said Joke Frog. "And they dropped a bunch of their stuff."

Leaving the the scraps and dropped items behind, the trio continued toward Swindon-on-Sea. Soon they could smell the sea air on the wind. That was normal when you walked to the ocean. But what *wasn't* normal was hearing a bunch of splashing. Which was exactly what they heard.

"What's that?" asked Pig Newton. "Sounds like sharks splashing around. But I don't think there are enough sharks in the sea to make that much noise."

After a little more walking they reached the hill where they could look down and see the sea. What they saw seemed to make no sense at all!

All the residents of Swindon were standing in the water. They were moving blocks and bricks and pieces of stone around. The bricks were being formed into buildings. The Swindonites did not look happy. In the water surrounding them, the sharks circled menacingly. Off to the side, Megalodon lounged at the edge of the water. An evil grin was spread across his face. His giant teeth glistened in the sunlight.

"Oh heck no!" said the Amazing Frog.

He began marching over toward Megalodon with long, purposeful strides. Pig Newton had never seen the Amazing Frog so angry. Usually, the Amazing Frog was a pretty laid back guy. He was fun-loving and enjoyed silly adventures. An angry Amazing Frog was going to be a whole new kettle of fish. Pig Newton decided to stay out of his way.

"Hey!" the Amazing Frog shouted. "Hey fish face!"

Megalodon looked over at the approaching amphibian. He continued to smile. If sharks had eyebrows—which they don't—Megalodon's would have been arched evilly.

"Oh, hello Amazing Frog," Megalodon said with a grin. "Where have you been all this time? Important things have been happening while you were off doing whatever."

"You know *exactly* where I've been!" said the Amazing Frog. "I was rescuing a bunch of people from a castle that *you* built! And they were trapped inside because *you* tricked them!"

"A castle?" said Megalodon innocently. "That doesn't sound like me. That sounds more like something your friend Joke Frog over there might do."

"This has nothing to do with Joke Frog, and you know it!" said the Amazing Frog, standing in Megalodon's long shadow. "Now tell me what you're doing! Why are the citizens of Swindon wading around in the water and doing. . . Doing. . . What *are* they doing, anyway? It looks like they're doing construction work in the middle of the bay."

"Very perceptive, Amazing Frog," said Megalodon. "That's precisely what they're doing."

"Why?" the Amazing Frog asked. "I don't understand."

"Then let me explain," said Megalodon. "Perhaps your amazing-ness doesn't extend to your intellect, eh Amazing Frog? Could it be that you're a little overrated? Anyhow, being a shark is pretty awesome, and maybe the most awesome part is eating frogs. That's pretty easy to do because so many delicious frogs come to Swindon-on-Sea to ride jet skis and swim in the water—and all kinds of other things that are liable to get you eaten by a shark. The thing is, there are never *enough* visitors. It's a real problem for me and my sharky friends. There are *a bunch* of frogs to eat over in Swindon. But that creates two big problems for sharks. Problem number one is that it's really far away. Even when you're riding on a blimp, it sure does take a while to get there. And problem number two is that sharks don't do so well out of the water. We kind of run out of juice."

"I'm sorry for all your difficult problems," the Amazing Frog said sarcastically. Really, he did not feel sorry for the sharks at all.

"The good news is that I've solved both issues," Megalodon continued. "While you were off doing goodness-knows-what, the other sharks and I paid a visit to downtown Swindon. It was a very quick visit, but we were quite persuasive. We let everybody know that they could come with us back to Swindon-on-Sea and *build a new Swindon* here in the bay. . . or they could get eaten. Remarkably, all of them chose to come with us and participate in our little building project. And now, one day soon, we'll have our own Swindon here in the bay where we can swim up and chase around yummy frogs whenever we feel like it, and we won't have to deal with getting out of the water."

"You dastardly villain!" the Amazing Frog exclaimed. "If I had been in Swindon, I would have stopped you from doing this. I would have shot you and the other sharks with rocket launchers, or put exploding tanks in your mouths and set them off. It would have tuned all of you into sushi!"

"Yes," said Megalodon, still grinning evilly. "But you weren't. So you didn't."

His mind still reeling from this bad news, the Amazing Frog tried to figure out what to do next. No way was he going to let Megalodon relocate Swindon. Swindon was already in a great place. A bay sticking out into the sea was a lousy place for a city. Everybody knew that.

Still, the Amazing Frog understood that Megalodon's evil plot to move Swindon would be hard to undo. The city's population was trapped doing construction work while surrounded by circling sharks. The Amazing Frog tried to think of what he could offer Megalodon in exchange for letting everyone go. To an outsider, it might have looked like Megalodon already had everything he wanted. But the Amazing Frog quickly decided that there was something important that the evil fish still lacked.

"It looks like you really have pulled your plan off without a hitch," the Amazing Frog said to Megalodon. "It's just a shame that everybody's going to hate you from now on. And *nobody's* going to see you as the lawful, legal ruler of Swindon. They'll just think of you as that jerk who moved the city. For ever and ever, the residents of this new Swindon are just going to be plotting how they can get revenge on you."

The Amazing Frog looked up into Megalodon's face to see if his words had made an impact. It was quickly clear that they had. Megalodon frowned. A single tear formed in his right eye.

"I don't want everybody to hate me," Megalodon said. "And I don't want them to see me as a jerk. I'm a perfectly nice shark. I just want to make it easier for me to swim over and eat frogs whenever I'm in the mood. Is that so much to ask?"

"What you need is a way to make what you've done here *legitimate*," said the Amazing Frog. "To make the people of Swindon see you as their rightful new ruler."

"How can I do that?" asked Megalodon.

The Amazing Frog said: "I think a good start would be if the most famous and important frog in all of Swindon—or, let's be honest, the most famous and important frog in all the world—told everyone that you were a good leader who they should follow. Anybody can make frogs do construction work in the middle of a bay when there are a bunch of scary sharks circling them. But if the frogs supported you of their own free will, you wouldn't have to *make* them build your new Swindon. They'd *want* to do it!"

"They would?" asked Megalodon, almost unable to picture it. "That would be amazing!"

The Amazing Frog nodded.

"And they'd do that just because a popular frog said they should?"

The Amazing Frog nodded again.

"Wow," said Megalodon. "But where would I ever find a frog like that?"

The Amazing Frog cleared his throat.

"You?!" said Megalodon. "Of course! *You're* the most popular frog in all of Swindon. Even if you are always pulling pranks on people and causing accidents and stuff. Everybody likes the Amazing Frog. Would you really do that for me? Would you give me your public endorsement."

"Yes, of course," said the Amazing Frog, nodding brightly.

The giant shark could hardly believe his ear holes. His jaw dropped again—not in surprise, but in delight.

Then the Amazing Frog added: "If. . ."

"*If*?" said Megalodon. "If what?"

"*If* you beat me and Pig Newton and Joke Frog in the Swindon-on-Sea Olympics," said the Amazing Frog.

"I *knew* there'd be a catch," said Megalodon angrily. "What are the Swindon-on-Sea Olympics?"

"They're just some fun games I know," said the Amazing Frog. "They're games I bet sharks would be really good at too. You'll probably beat us easily."

"Oh yeah?" asked Megalodon suspiciously.

"Yeah," said the Amazing Frog. "But here's the thing: If we beat you, then you have to agree to let all the frogs go back to Swindon—the real one."

"Hmm," said Megalodon, considering carefully. "That sounds risky, but it's a risk I'm willing to take. You're on!"

The Amazing Frog was secretly pleased. It looked like the battle was not over yet. They still had a chance to save the people of Swindon.

"Very good," said the Amazing Frog. "Let me have a word with Pig Newton and Joke Frog, and we'll get things set up. In the meantime, you should get all the Swindon frogs out of the water."

"And why should I do that?" asked Megalodon.

"Because we're going to need the bay for our Olympic events," answered the Amazing Frog. "Plus, they can be our audience."

And with that, the Amazing Frog bounded back over to his friends to tell them the exciting news.

The Swindon-on-Sea Olympics were about to begin!

## Chapter Seven

"I don't know about this," said Pig Newton. "I'm a pig, after all. We're not exactly known for being good at athletics. In fact, our bodies are kind of designed to be *the opposite* of what you need to be good at sports. We have these big round torsos and little tiny legs!"

"Relax," said the Amazing Frog. "I promise you won't have to compete in anything that isn't suited to your. . . um. . . unique bodily proportions."

"Well that's a relief," said Pig Newton. "What's the first event going to be?"

"I was thinking the high jump," said the Amazing Frog. "That's a traditional Olympic event. There's no way Megalodon can have any problem with it. And don't worry. I'll be the first competitor."

"Sounds goods to me," said Pig Newton. "I can't jump very high at all. Hey Joke Frog, are you any good at jumping?"

"Only when it's part of a really bad punchline," Joke Frog said. "Like jumping to conclusions or something."

The Amazing Frog swam back out to the center of the bay where Megalodon was waiting. The frogs from Swindon had stopped their work and gathered on the shore. They sat in orderly rows, a little unsure what was going on, but excited to be watching Olympic events. Plus, it was more fun than doing construction work.

"Okay," said Megalodon. "Everything's set up like you asked. Now what's the first event?"

"I was thinking the high jump," said the Amazing Frog.

"Pssh," said Megalodon dismissively. "An event that clearly favors frogs. Typical."

"Wait," said the Amazing Frog. "I know a way to make it fair for everyone. We'll see who can jump the highest. . . *out of the water*."

"Out of the water, eh?" said Megalodon. "So, if you were a shark, say. . . you could dive down below, build up some momentum, and breach out of the water as high as you could?"

The Amazing Frog nodded.

"And frogs wouldn't be able to push-off from anything. . . like a trampoline, for example?"

"Absolutely not," said the Amazing Frog.

"Done!" said Megalodon. "And you're going to regret it. This is an event where the sharks are sure to win!"

"Fine," said the Amazing Frog. "Now if you'll excuse me for a moment, I need to go change into my swimming trunks."

"Whatever," said Megalodon. "Just hurry up. I'm excited to beat you by jumping way higher than you do!"

The Amazing Frog hurried off to one of the portable toilets that lined the beach. He went inside and closed the door.

The Amazing Frog had long found that portable toilets were a great place to stash weapons when he wasn't using them. The beach toilets at Swindon-on-Sea were no exception. The Amazing Frog reached behind the toilet to where a number of weapons were stashed. He felt around until his webby fingers touched a long thick barrel that was pointed at one end. The Amazing Frog's lips curled into a grin. He gripped the weapon and stuck it down the back of his swimming trunks. Then he left the portable toilet and dove back into the water, concealing the weapon.

He swam up to Megalodon, who looked impatient.

"Are you ready now?" Megalodon asked in an annoyed voice.

"Sure am," said the Amazing Frog. "But why don't you go first? It's my event that I picked out, so you should have the honor of making the first try."

"Fine," said Megalodon confidently. "But back up. I'm going to be going pretty fast when I come out of the water. I wouldn't want any puny little frogs to get hurt."

The shark grinned evilly. Then he dove down and disappeared beneath the water.

The Amazing Frog dog-paddled off to the side, giving Megalodon the whole bay to himself.

The audience watched expectantly, wondering what would happen next. The water across the top of the bay was as still as glass. Nothing happened.

At first.

Then a great shadow suddenly became visible beneath the water. It got larger and larger as everyone looked. The Amazing Frog realized the shadow was Megalodon propelling himself upward toward the surface of the water. A moment later, the huge shark shot out of the water and up into the air. It used its powerful tail muscles to give itself one last push as it shot from the bay. Megalodon flew so high that for a moment he blocked out the sun. The Amazing Frog squinted in surprise as he was thrust into the shade. When Megalodon had flown a full hundred feet into the air, his momentum finally ceased, and he began to fall back down. The great shark hit the water with a belly-flop that the Amazing Frog was pretty sure was intentional. It sent a great wave of water splashing over the audience on the beach. It was such an impressive sight, that, for a moment, only a hushed silence followed.

Then there was a cascade of applause.

"Why is everybody applauding?!" said Pig Newton. "Don't they know he's the guy who kidnapped them and forced them to come here?"

"Megalodon might be a jerk, but dang—a good jump is a good jump," opined Joke Frog.

Megalodon surfaced and swam confidently to the shoreline.

"I like these 'Olympics,'" said Megalodon. "Maybe I should be a full-time Olympic athlete."

"It's hard to do that," said Pig Newton. "The Olympics only happen once every four years. Or when a town gets kidnapped, I guess."

Megalodon looked down his nose at Pig Newton, as though he were trying to decide whether to devour the pig in a single bite. Pig Newton decided he wouldn't point out any other facts about the Olympics to Megalodon.

Next, it was the Amazing Frog's turn to jump. He swam to the center of the bay and ducked down beneath the waterline. The audience quieted.

"What do you think he's going to do?" Pig Newton asked Joke Frog. "There's no way he can jump as high as Megalodon. He doesn't have big fins or powerful tail muscles or anything like that."

"No," said Joke Frog thoughtfully. "He tends to have other stuff, though. After all, he's the Amazing Frog."

"I hope he has something that can help him jump really high," Pig Newton said. "Otherwise, we're in big trouble!"

The Amazing Frog swam down, as deep as he could go. When he reached the bottom of the bay, he touched his feet against the sea floor and used his legs to push himself upwards like a rocket. The Amazing Frog flew upward and burst through the surface of the water. His momentum carried him into the air. . .about three feet into the air.

"Oh no!" Pig Newton just had time to exclaim. "He's not going to-"

Then a very surprising thing happened. (At least it was surprising to Pig Newton, who didn't know that the Amazing Frog had grabbed a rocket launcher and stuck it down the back of his pants.)

The Amazing Frog pulled the trigger on the rocket launcher. The rocket was pointing down, toward the water. There was a tremendous 'whooshing' sound as it took off. When it did, the momentum from the rocket shot the Amazing Frog high into the air. Gripping the rocket launcher, the Amazing Frog was carried up until he was just a tiny spot against the sun—several hundred feet into the air. Then he slowed his ascent and reversed his trajectory, falling back to the bay with a triumphant belly flop. His splash—when he landed—was nowhere as large as Megalodon's, but it was still pretty impressive.

There was a moment of surprised silence, but then the audience broke out into enthusiastic applause. It was twice as loud as they had applauded for Megalodon.

"Wow!" said Pig Newton. "That was awesome!"

"See, he always has something up his sleeve," said Joke Frog.

The Amazing Frog swam over to Megalodon.

"No hard feelings, big guy," the Amazing Frog said. "But I think it's clear that I won."

"I didn't know you were going to shoot an RPG out of your butt," said Megalodon. "If I had, I wouldn't have agreed to this event. Now I think this Olympics-thing is stupid. I don't want to be an athlete anymore!"

The Amazing Frog knew that if Megalodon decided to stop participating in their little contest, it would be difficult to find another way to rescue the people of Swindon. He had to keep the giant shark interested.

"Why don't *you* pick the next event?" the Amazing Frog said to Megalodon. "It can be anything you like!"

Even as he said these words, the Amazing Frog cringed inside. He knew that Megalodon was a mean jerk, and that the shark would probably devise some sort of mean-spirited and unpleasant event. As it turned out, the Amazing Frog was correct.

"Hmm," said Megalodon. "Let me think of something. . . good."

For his part, Megalodon was trying to think of an event that would be impossible for a shark to lose. . . or impossible for a frog to win. Even if he *did* have a rocket launcher down his pants. (And if this next event hurt or annoyed people in the process, so much the better! Megalodon liked be a jerk.)

"Okay," Megalodon finally said. "I've got it. The aim of the next event will be to give people a ride though the water. A very *rough ride.* In fact, the object will be to see how sick and nauseated you can make the people sitting on your back."

"Ooh, that Megalodon is evil!" said Pig Newton when he heard this.

"We'll decide on who is the winner based on how much the people riding on your back throw-up!" announced Megalodon for a disgusting grand finale.

The Amazing Frog was not so sure about this. He needed to keep Megalodon engaged, but this felt like it crossed some kind of line.

"Wait a minute, Megalodon," the Amazing Frog said. "I don't know if I can agree to this. First of all, just think about the logistics. I mean, you're a big shark that can fit lots of people on your back. How is a frog supposed to fit more than a handful of people?"

"That's *your* problem, isn't it?" said Megalodon.

"It just doesn't seem fair," said the Amazing Frog. "I don't think-"

But the Amazing Frog was stopped mid-sentence by Joke Frog.

Joke Frog leaned in and quietly whispered something into the Amazing Frog's ear.

The Amazing Frog looked surprised. He turned to look Joke Frog square in the face, to see if the painted amphibian was serious.

"Are you *sure*?" the Amazing Frog asked. "You really think that will work?"

Joke Frog nodded confidently.

"Well, okay," said the Amazing Frog. "It's worth a shot."

The Amazing Frog turned his attention back to Megalodon, who waited expectantly.

"Okay, Megalodon," the Amazing Frog said. "We agree. We'll do this event . . . even if it will mean making a lot of people throw up. Also, you're gross for thinking of this."

Megalodon smiled. He liked being gross. The Amazing Frog could tell.

"All right," Megalodon said. "I'm going to go first. This time, I'm sure I'll win!"

Megalodon swam up to the beach where the audience of frogs from Swindon was waiting.

"Get on my back, as many of you as can fit!" the evil shark commanded.

About ten frogs reluctantly climbed onto his back.

Laden with this cargo, Megalodon swam over to the Swindon-on-Sea docks where the construction equipment had been piled. Among it were buckets used for carrying rocks and other heavy things. Megalodon eyed them intently.

"Each one of you, grab a bucket!" the shark shouted to his passengers.

Dutifully, each one of the frogs grabbed a bucket. They didn't know exactly where the shark was planning on taking them, but they all felt like it definitely wasn't going to be a fun trip.

"And don't drop those buckets during the ride!" Megalodon snapped. "If you do, then I won't get credit for it."

"Credit for what?" one of the frogs had the courage to ask.

"For your throw-up," the shark said with a sinister gleam in his eye, and pushed off into the bay.

Megalodon began swimming in a long, slow circle around the bay. At first he did not go much faster than a standard motorboat. Some of the frogs on his back even found the ride fun.

"Ooh, I quite like this," one of the frogs said to her neighbor. "This is like taking a boat tour. The wind is quite invigorating!"

Then Megalodon kicked it up a notch. The great shark began swimming faster and faster. Soon, he was creating so much wake behind him that it was hard to see his enormous tailfin. When maximum speed had been achieved, Megalodon began to add twists and turns to his routine. He flipped and flopped over the water. And all the while, he made his circle in the bay tighter and tighter.

"Ugh," one of the frogs said. "This isn't like a fun boat tour anymore. This is more like being on a ride at an amusement park that's going far too fast and out of control! In fact, I'm afraid I'm going to. . . Going to. . ."

But the frog could not finish her sentence. This was because she was too busy filling up the bottom of her bucket. Then her neighbors started throwing up too. (Frog barf is especially gross because of what frogs eat, which is mostly flies and other insects. When a bunch of half-digested flies comes back up, nobody's very happy about it.)

Megalodon continued to circle tighter and tighter. He wanted to squeeze every drop he could out of his passengers. Soon, many of the frogs began turning green with nausea—which was remarkable because they were already kind of green anyway. Megalodon thought for sure that he had won.

When it seemed the poor frogs had had all that they could take, Megalodon slowed and turned back toward the shore. The frogs on his back looked very relieved by this turn of events, but still quite sick. After a ride like that, they were going to feel poorly for a while!

Megalodon piloted himself back to the dock where there was an industrial scale used for weighing concrete. He pulled up beside it and stopped.

"All of you, get off my back and stack your buckets on the scale!" commanded Megalodon. "And don't spill anything. . . or I'll have to take you out again!"

The idea of a second ride was enough to instill fear in the heads of every one of the frogs. They carefully dismounted and gingerly carried their puke-buckets up to the enormous scale. They stacked the buckets one atop the other until they formed a pyramid. When the last frog had set her bucket on the scale, everyone watched the needle. It settled right at twenty pounds.

"Ha!" said Megalodon happily. "Even better than I thought I'd do. Twenty pounds of puke!"

"Well, the buckets weigh something too," Pig Newton whispered to the Amazing Frog.

"Excuse me?" said Megalodon sharply. "What was that?"

"Erm, nothing," said Pig Newton.

"That's what I thought," said the shark. "Now, Amazing Frog, it's your team's turn. See if you can beat twenty pounds of puke."

"Okay," said the Amazing Frog confidently. "Joke Frog is going to participate in this event on behalf of our team."

"Fine," Megalodon said. "Just get on with it."

The Amazing Frog turned to look into Joke Frog's painted face.

"All right, buddy," the Amazing Frog said. "Your plan had better work."

"Relax," said Joke Frog. "I've got it all under control."

Joke Frog waded into the water and paddled over to the frog audience.

"I need some volunteers," said Joke Frog. "Climb onto my back, as many as can fit."

"But you'll make us puke!" said one of the frogs. "We just saw what Megalodon did. We're not stupid."

"Do you want to maybe puke a little now, or do you want to have to rebuild Swindon out here in the water and be a slave to the sharks forever?" Joke Frog asked. "Which is worse?"

"Hmm, I see your point," one of the frogs replied, and began clamoring aboard Joke Frog's back.

Joke Frog was smaller than Megalodon. Much smaller. Where Megalodon had been able to fit ten frogs quite comfortably, Joke Frog could only fit four. And those four were smooshed together very tightly.

Joke Frog began to slowly paddle over to the stack of buckets. He couldn't go very fast with four other frogs sitting on his back.

"Haha!" laughed Megalodon, watching from the sidelines. "He can only carry four frogs! So just to *tie* me, he's got to make each of them puke five pounds each. Good luck with that!"

Joke Frog ignored Megalodon. Once his passengers had their buckets, Joke Frog swam out to the center of the bay. He started swimming in circles. However, his circles were much wider—and his pace was much slower—than Megalodon's had been. He wasn't creating a very rough ride for his passengers.

"Oh, this is going to be a massacre!" Megalodon exclaimed with glee. "I'm going to beat you guys so bad! Joke Frog will be lucky if he squeezes one drop out of those frogs!"

Joke Frog ignored this cruel taunting and continued circling.

Pig Newton felt so worried that he could hardly bear to watch.

"Should we just give up?" Pig Newton whispered to the Amazing Frog. "Joke Frog's just embarrassing himself. It seems there's no hope of him getting those frogs to puke. He's too small and slow!"

The Amazing Frog shook his head.

"No, we shouldn't give up, Pig Newton," replied the Amazing Frog. "Give Joke Frog a chance. Sometimes if you give people a chance, they can really surprise you."

"Oh," Pig Newton said. "Okay. I'll wait and see what he can do."

Joke Frog continued to circle in the middle of the bay. Try as he might, he just couldn't generate enough speed to make anybody feel sick, or even uncomfortable. To an onlooker like Pig Newton, it actually seemed like he was giving them a very pleasant ride.

"Hahaha," said Megalodon. "It's over! Throw in the towel!"

Then something remarkable happened. One of the frogs on Joke Frog's back began throwing up into his bucket. Pig Newton looked at the Amazing Frog in surprise. The Amazing Frog flashed the tiniest hint of a smile with the corner of his mouth.

"Ehh, that could be a coincidence," said Megalodon. "Maybe that frog is just prone to seasickness. Or he ate a bad fly before. Could happen to anybody. I'm not worried."

Yet no sooner were these words out of Megalodon's enormous mouth than a second frog began throwing up into his bucket. Then a third. Then they were all throwing up. . . and throwing up a lot! Megaldon couldn't believe his eyes.

After a few minutes of this, Joke Frog changed course and started paddling back to the dock.

"Gee, I guess he's done and he can't make them throw up any more," Pig Newton theorized.

"Maybe," said the Amazing Frog. "But I think their buckets are just full. He could make them throw up even more if he wanted to, but it'd just be a waste of time!"

Pig Newton looked closer and saw that the Amazing Frog was right. As Joke Frog pulled up to the dock and the passenger-frogs woozily got off his back, they had trouble carrying the buckets because they were so full. When they stacked the buckets on the scale, they weighed twenty-one pounds—a pound more than all the buckets from Megalodon's passengers! Megalodon's face fell. He could hardly believe it. Joke Frog strode confidently back over to the Amazing Frog and Pig Newton.

"Wow!" said Pig Newton. "That was incredible. But how did you do it? It looked like you were just paddling around slowly."

"I was," said Joke Frog. "But while I was doing that, I was telling gross jokes."

"Gross jokes?" asked Pig Newton.

Joke Frog nodded.

"Of course. Every humorist like me needs to have some gross jokes in his repertoire. Like, for example, have you heard about the dead zombie frog, whose eyes were rotting out of his head and his guts were falling out and his skin smelled like rotting meat—because *it was* rotting meat—and his-"

"We get the idea, Joke Frog," the Amazing Frog said.

"But I didn't even finish the setup," Joke Frog said.

"That's okay," said Pig Newton. "I was already starting to throw up in my mouth a little bit. I never thought I'd say this, but I'm glad you know some good gross jokes, Joke Frog."

It was at this moment that Megalodon swam over. His surprise had turned to anger. Sharks didn't need to breathe in the same way frogs and pigs did, but Megalodon was huffing and puffing just to seem extra-intimidating.

"I don't know how you did that, but I'm sure it wasn't fair!" he cried. "You guys cheated. Or used magic. Or cheated *and then* used magic."

"We did nothing of the kind, and you know it," the Amazing Frog said. "Now be polite, or I won't tell you about the next event. You still want to win an event, don't you?"

Megalodon fell silent. It was clear that he very much did.

"This next event is easy," the Amazing Frog assured the giant shark. "Because all you have to do is stand still."

"Okay," Megalodon said. "I can do tha-"

"*Completely* still," added the Amazing Frog. "While the other team is trying to distract you."

"Oh," said Megalodon. "I get it. I bet I can totally do that."

"Here," said the Amazing Frog. "We'll hold this event over by the frog audience so they can be the judge of who wins and who loses."

"I'm going to win this one," said Megalodon. "I'm due. I can feel it."

Megalodon confidently swam over to the spot on the beach where the crowd was sitting. As they walked over to join Megalodon, the Amazing Frog turned to Pig Newton.

"Okay, Pig Newton," he said. "It's your time to shine. You'll be representing our team in this event!"

"Me?" said Pig Newton. "Why me?"

"Because you're so good at standing still," said the Amazing Frog. "Whenever I come to find you, you're always just standing around, right?"

"I *do* stand around a lot," Pig Newton admitted.

"And you're also good at not getting distracted," the Amazing Frog assured him. "Like, half the time when I'm talking to you, and I'm telling you we need to do something or go somewhere, you don't even listen. You don't even hear what I literally just told you a moment ago. And that's because you're so good at not getting distracted by me."

"Wow!" said Pig Newton. "I thought that was a trait of mine that annoyed you. But now it's totally gonna pay off."

"It *does* annoy me, Pig Newton," said the Amazing Frog. "But you're correct. Your ability to be forgetful and distracted is going to be an asset in this situation. In fact, I can't think of anybody I know who is better at those things than you are."

"Gee, you've really filled me with confidence!" Pig Newton said. "I can beat Megalodon in this event. I just know it! I never thought I'd be able to beat Megalodon at anything. . . except possibly a being-eaten-by-Megalodon contest."

They reached the edge of the water where the giant shark was preparing himself.

"I went first in the last two events," Megalodon reminded them. "This time, *your* team should go first."

"Fine," the Amazing Frog said. "Our contestant will be Pig Newton here. Pig Newton, you can start whenever you're ready. Megalodon, you can do anything you like to try to distract him, but you can't touch him."

"Or eat him," Pig Newton added.

"Eating would involve touching something, now wouldn't it, Pig Newton?" the Amazing Frog said.

"Yeah, I guess you're right," Pig Newton said. "No touching probably covers it."

"I'll set a timer on my phone for two minutes," said the Amazing Frog. "Aaaaaand go!"

Pig Newton stood stock still. He tried to clear his mind. Luckily for him, his mind was always clear, so this was just a matter of reverting back to his default setting. Pig Newton's mind was like an empty pool of mud that nobody had began to wallow in yet. It was flat and dark and still. Which was just the way he liked it.

Pig Newton stood on the edge of the beach, and Megalodon hovered several feet away in the shallow water.

"Roar!" cried Megalodon. "I'm a big scary shark and I'm going to eat you. I know we just said that I wouldn't do that but. . . . roar!!! I'm gonna do it anyway!!!"

Megalodon gnashed his giant knifey teeth and opened his mouth as wide as it would go, which was very wide indeed. Several Pig Newtons could have fit easily inside. Pig Newton could see all the way down Megalodon's throat to where fish—who had met their end earlier that day—were being digested.

Even though this was a frightening sight, Pig Newton did not flinch. His mind stayed focused on the pool of mud in his mind. He ignored the scary shark.

Seeing that being frightening wasn't going to work, Megalodon decided to take a different tack.

"Okay, Pig Newton. . . this is you," the shark said, and began talking in a high-pitched, annoying voice. "I'm Pig Newton and I'm a big nerd. I do whatever the Amazing Frog says. I spend all my time standing around doing nothing because I'm so boring. I can't swim around or eat people like a big cool shark can. I'm so very, very uncool."

The shark's insults bounced off of Pig Newton. His little pig brain was far away, locked in Zen-like fantasy of the perfect mud puddle.

More time ran out. Megalodon began to fear he would get no reaction out of Pig Newton at all. He began to taunt more desperately.

"You know what else is stupid about me?" the shark continued in a mocking voice. "I play in mud puddles and wallow around in dirty, stinky mud. I actually think mud is a good thing, when most people understand that mud is something you go out of your way to *avoid.* Who wants to get muddy?  I'll tell you who. Nobody. Nobody, except maybe a dirty, filthy, silly-"

Pig Newton had had enough.

"You can say anything you want to about *me*!" the pig cried. "But leave the mud out of it!  Leave the mud alone!"

Megalodon grinned with glee. His taunting had worked.

"Aaaand time," said the Amazing Frog, consulting the clock on his phone. "Darn it, Pig Newton. You stumbled right at the finish line, so to speak. Megalodon got a rise out of you at the last moment."

"I don't care!" Pig Newton replied defensively. "Insulting me is one thing, but insulting mud goes too far.

What did mud ever do? Except keep pigs cool in the summer, and warm in the winter, and protect us from mosquitoes and biting insects, and feel like a nice squishy blanket you get to wear all the time. . . oh, how I love mud!"

The Amazing Frog rolled his eyes.

"Okay," cried the huge shark. "My turn! My turn!"

"Fine," said the Amazing Frog. "You've got to hold still for two minutes. The only rule is we're not allowed to touch you. I'll start the timer. Aaaaaand go."

At his spot near the beach, Megalodon abruptly went as motionless as a statue. He was very good at it. His head was sticking above the waterline, but he left his gill slits in the water so he could breathe. (After all, it was a standing still contest, not a breath holding contest.) Megalodon looked just like a stuffed shark on display in a museum. It was really quite eerie.

Immediately, the Amazing Frog, Joke Frog, and Pig Newton set out to make Megalodon lose his composure.

Pig Newton said: "Look at me, I'm Megalodon. I'm a big stupid shark and everybody hates me. Nyah nyah nyah."

And he danced around the beach in front of Megalodon.

"How many big, stupid sharks does it take to change a light bulb?" joked Joke Frog. "None. Because the big, stupid shark got exploded when someone put a compression tank in his mouth and then shot it with a rifle, and then the shark exploded and turned into sushi, and everybody knows that *sushi can't change light bulbs*!"

Neither of these taunts worked. Megalodon remained stock still. The time on the Amazing Frog's watch ticked by. He realized that they needed to take another approach, and fast!

Instead of going up to Megalodon, the Amazing Frog walked over to where the residents of Swindon were gathered—watching expectantly, as if their fates hung in the balance. . .which indeed they did!

"Okay!" the Amazing Frog said loudly—loud enough for Megalodon to hear. "Now that Megalodon's frozen still for two minutes. . . everybody, follow me. We're going to hightail it before he can stop us! I know a castle up the coastline where we can hide. Hurry. Let's get a head start before the sharks can follow!"

"Noooo!" came a great and deep bellow. "You will all stay exactly where you are! Do as I say or you will be eaten!"

Megalodon used his giant fins to push himself up the beach and glower intimidatingly over the citizens of Swindon.

A moment later, he realized what he had done.

"Oh *darn it*!" Megalodon cried.

"Ha ha, got you!" cried Pig Newton.

"Joke's on you . . . you lost!" said Joke Frog.

"And we made you break your composure much faster than Pig Newton did," said the Amazing Frog, checking his timer. "It looks like we win this event too!"

"No fair!" Megalodon said angrily. "You can't tell people they can leave and go to the castle!"

"The rules were we can do anything except touch you," said the Amazing Frog. "We won fair and square."

Megalodon frowned.

"This makes me not want to play these Olympic games at all," Megalodon said. "I'm down zero-to-three.

Maybe I shouldn't play anymore. Maybe I should just eat everybody."

"Now, now," said the Amazing Frog. "You don't want to be known as a quitter, do you?"

"No," said Megalodon. " I guess not."

"Then try doing just one more event," encouraged the Amazing Frog. "This one can be winner-take-all. It'll give you a fresh start."

"That sounds nice," Megalodon said. "Okay. One final Olympic event. What did you you have in mind?"

The Amazing Frog knew he had to be careful. Even if they defeated Megalodon fair and square, it was looking less and less likely that he would honor their agreement. The Amazing Frog considered what to do carefully. The fate of all the citizens of Swindon hung in the balance.

"I think we should play another classic game," the Amazing Frog eventually said. "One that you've probably played since you were a tiny baby shark. You *were* tiny once upon a time, right?"

"Relatively speaking," confirmed Megalodon. "A tiny Megalodon is still much bigger than you."

"Well now we're going to play something you've probably played since you were that size," said the Amazing Frog. "We're going to play hide and seek!"

Megalodon's eyes shifted back and forth rapidly. The great shark was trying to decide whether it liked this idea or not.

"So can I, for example, hide underneath the sea?" asked Megalodon cagily.

"I don't see why you couldn't," the Amazing Frog replied. "We should set the boundaries as Swindon-on-Sea, but other than that, there are no limitations."

Megalodon's eyes went back and forth again. He was picturing all of his favorite hiding spots located deep in the sea's craggy bottom.

"Hmmm," said Megalodon. "It sounds like an awfully tempting contest..."

The Amazing Frog could see that Megalodon was nearly at the point of agreeing.

"Tell you what," said the Amazing Frog. "If it will make it an easier decision for you, I'll sweeten the deal. We'll decide who wins by how long it takes the hiding team to be found. But here's the thing. All three of us—me, Joke Frog, and Pig Newton—will hide. And when you find any of the three of us, it counts as finding all of us. But only I will come looking for you. As I see it, you'll get a three-to-one advantage over us."

The shark's eyes went back and forth some more. Then they became still again. And focused intently on the Amazing Frog.

"Agreed," said Megalodon. "This final contest is going to be the most exciting of all!"

Pig Newton sidled up beside the Amazing Frog.

"What are you *doing*?" the pig whispered. "That's too much of an advantage. He'll beat us this time for sure!"

"Quiet!" the Amazing Frog whispered back. "I have a plan. Trust me."

Megalodon stuck his giant head in closer, to interrupt their conversation.

"I want to have the first shot at seeking," Megalodon asserted. "I think the three of you are going to be *very* easy to find. Amazing Frog, I suppose you *might* blend in with the greenish water. . . but Pig Newton's big pink belly is going to make his very easy to find. And do I even have to mention Joke Frog? With his bright white face and purple jacket, he'll stick out like a sore thumb! A *purple* sore thumb!"

"We'll see about that," the Amazing Frog said. "Now put your fin over your eyes and count to a hundred."

"Okay," said the shark.

He covered his eyes and began counting.

"One. . . two. . . three. . . Four. . . ."

The final game was afoot!

## Chapter Eight

"I don't see why we have to do it this way," whispered Pig Newton. "If you ask me, it makes no sense."

The three of them were huddled together behind at rock at the side of the bay. They were waist-deep in the water. The Amazing Frog had one arm around Pig Newton, and the other around Joke Frog. While his embrace was mostly friendly, Pig Newton had the distinct feeling that the Amazing Frog would have no problem physically restraining him if he tried to swim away.

"I already told you why we're doing it this way," the Amazing Frog said testily. "It makes it harder for Megalodon to find us. If we're in three different places, he can stumble upon any of the three places. And then he's won. But if we're all in the same place, then he can only win if he looks for us in one place—in this case, here behind this rock."

"Hmm," said Pig Newton. "I *guess* that makes sense. Kinda. But I still think it's a little weird."

"Look, are you an expert at hiding?" asked the Amazing Frog.

"No," said Pig Newton. "In fact, I'm probably really easy to find. I'm always standing in a real easy-to-see location, like the middle of a field."

"Exactly," said the Amazing Frog. "Now be quiet. It's almost time."

From the other side of the bay, they heard Megalodon finish counting down.

"Ninety-eight. . . ninety-nine. . . ONE HUNDRED! HERE I COME!"

There was a splash as Megalodon cast off into the water and began combing the bay. Then there was only silence. Megalodon had dived down like a submarine. He was cruising under the water.

Pig Newton looked over at the Amazing Frog nervously, wondering what was going to happen. Joke Frog also looked around. Joke Frog seemed less nervous, and more annoyed that the need for silence was preventing him from telling the latest joke that had popped into his head. The Amazing Frog did his best to keep both of them quiet.

For a couple of minutes, nothing happened. Nothing stirred. But then, quite abruptly, the Amazing Frog noticed a large, dark shape in the water nearby. The shape seemed to come from the bottom of the sea itself, and it was growing closer and closer. This had to be Megalodon.

The Amazing Frog put a single slender finger to the side of his nostril, indicating to his friends that they should be very quiet indeed.

The giant shape moved closer, and closer still.

Pig Newton found this made him too nervous to watch, and he hid his hands in his hooves.

Then a remarkable thing happened. The giant shadow came near to the rock where they were hiding. . . and moved past. The shape did not even pause or hesitate. It did not investigate the rock at all. It merely crept up the coastline.

The Amazing Frog couldn't believe his luck. What a relief!  He began to relax. Then he relaxed even more. So did Pig Newton and Joke Frog.

Then there was a surprising noise.

"Pfffffffffft!"

It was followed by several small bubbles that floated to the top of the water—one by one—around the Amazing Frog's legs.

The dark shadow underneath the water suddenly paused in its progress up the coast.

"What was *that*?" said Pig Newton.

"Um, that was me," the Amazing Frog admitted. "Sometimes I fart when I get relaxed. Usually, it's an advantage because I can use it to jump higher. But it's not an advantage in this situation."

No sooner were these words out of the Amazing Frog's mouth than the great shadow headed straight for their hiding place behind the rock. Megalodon emerged from the water with a mighty roar.

"Found you!" he cried.

"Yeah, yeah, you got us," said the Amazing Frog. "Okay. Fair's fair."

"How did you know we were here?" asked Pig Newton. "Did you hear the Amazing Frog farting?"

"Unfortunately, I smelled it!" said Megalodon, wrinkling his nose. "Sharks have amazing senses of smell. We can smell a single drop of blood in the middle of ocean. So we can definitely smell one of the Amazing Frog's gross frog-farts."

"Hey," said Joke Frog. "Frog farts aren't any worse than shark farts. That actually reminds me of a shark joke. What do you call a shark that's all by itself? Give up? A-lone shark! Get it? Like, a loan shark?"

"Wow!" said Megalodon. "I've heard some bad shark jokes before—being a shark and all—but that takes the cake!"

"Okay," said the Amazing Frog. "It's your turn to hide, Megalodon."

The giant shark's eyes gleamed. It was clear Megalodon had a super-secret hiding spot in mind. He had been waiting for this moment. The Amazing Frog had little doubt that it would be a carefully-guarded nook or cranny, deep beneath the ocean.

"Yes," said Megalodon. "I'll go and hide now, while the three of you count to one hundred. And remember, this is the deciding event. You've got to find me faster than I found you."

"Yeah, yeah," said the Amazing Frog. "Just get to hiding. We're counting now. One. . . Two. . . Three. . ."

As the Amazing Frog, Pig Newton, and Joke Frog covered their eyes and began to count, Megalodon submerged beneath the water and disappeared far beneath Swindon-on-Sea.

A few seconds later, the Amazing Frog risked a peek from behind his fingers. Megalodon was gone. There was not even a shadow beneath the water.

"Sixteen. . . Seventeen. . . Eighteen. . ." counted Pig Newton.

"Okay, you can stop now," said the Amazing Frog.

Pig Newton looked aghast.

"Stop? But if I do that, I'll forget where I am. Then I'll have to start all over again to get to one hundred."

"We're not counting to one hundred," asserted the Amazing Frog. "You can stop counting too, Joke Frog."

"But I know so many number jokes!" Joke Frog said. "Like why is six afraid of seven. Because seven *ate* nine!"

"We're not going to count to a hundred, and we're definitely not going to spend all afternoon looking for Megalodon at the bottom of the sea. He's hiding in one of a thousand seafloor fissures, and finding him would be like looking for a needle in a haystack."

"That doesn't sound very fun," said Pig Newton. "What if you got poked by the needle? And hay can be sharp sometimes, too. I would stay out of the haystack entirely."

"Riiiight," said the Amazing Frog, rolling his eyes. "That's why what we're going to do is get everybody from Swindon to race back to the city with us. By the time Megalodon thinks he's won and surfaces, we'll be long gone. And so will all of the citizens he captured."

"Oh," said Pig Newton. "But isn't that cheating?"

"Was it cheating when Megalodon captured all these frogs in the first place, and forced them to come to Swindon-on-Sea?" asked the Amazing Frog.

"That was way worse than cheating," Pig Newton said. "I think I see your point."

"Besides, we've already beaten Megalodon at three events," said the Amazing Frog. "He's crazy if he thinks he's going to win at this point. Now, let's hurry!"

The Amazing Frog took off across the beach until he reached the assembled citizens of Swindon. They were looking on curiously and eagerly, trying to understand what was happening. The Amazing Frog wasted no time in addressing them.

"Listen up, everybody," he said. "Here's our one chance! We need to hightail it back to Swindon while Megalodon is hidden underneath the water. If we all hurry as fast as we can, I think we can reach the city before he knows what's happened. And by the time he's figured it out, we'll be ready for him."

The frogs didn't have to be told twice. They jumped up and began sprinting back in the direction of Swindon. It was like watching a herd of cattle moving all at once. The frogs spread out across the plain in a great green blob, and headed as fast as they could toward the city.

The Amazing Frog prepared to join them, but Pig Newton sidled up beside him first.

"Hey," Pig Newton said. "What did you mean when you said 'We'll be ready for him' when Megalodon figures it out? Ready for what? What's he going to do?"

"Honestly, I don't exactly know," said the Amazing Frog. "But considering Megalodon's temperament, it's going to be something very bad indeed."

"Uh oh," said Pig Newton. "I'm suddenly feeling very concerned."

"Don't worry too much," said the Amazing Frog. "Things will be different if the sharks attack Swindon this time. For one, I'll be there!"

"If you'll be with us, then I don't feel scared or concerned," said Pig Newton. "In fact, I feel ready for anything Megalodon wants to throw at us. Bring it on, you big ugly fish!"

"That's the spirit," said the Amazing Frog, and they hurried back to Swindon together.

## Chapter Nine

The Amazing Frog glared hard through the binoculars, studying the rocky horizon with all his might. The binoculars were focused in the direction of Swindon-on-Sea. He knew this was where the shark assault was likely to originate.

The Amazing Frog was at the very top of the tallest building in downtown Swindon. Arrayed next to him were all of his favorite weapons—a rocket launcher, a machine gun, a laser gun, and even a water gun just in case it should be useful.

Pig Newton and Joke Frog huddled beside the Amazing Frog. The other citizens of Swindon took up defensive positions wherever they could. The Amazing Frog had ordered the cars—that were usually spread out all over the downtown area—to be moved to form barriers so that they might block any sharks who tried to come careening down the streets. Other openings had been similarly fortified.

Pig Newton watched the Amazing Frog as he looked through his binoculars.

"What are you looking for?" asked Pig Newton. "Shark fins on the horizon?"

"Maybe," said the Amazing Frog. "I'm looking for anything out of the ordinary. A bunch of fins coming this way would certainly count, I think."

"Megalodon's going to be really mad when he figures out what we did," said Pig Newton.

"Well that's his fault, isn't it?" said the Amazing Frog. "We only stole-back the citizens of Swindon because he stole them in the first place. It's all his doing, if you ask me. He brought this on himself."

Then Joke Frog said: "How do you stop a giant shark who's really, really angry with you?"

"How?" said the Amazing Frog and Pig Newton at the same time.

"I dunno," said Joke Frog. "That's not a joke. I'm asking because I'm honestly curious."

The Amazing Frog smiled at his friends.

"It's good to be well-prepared, but you guys are a little too nervous," the Amazing Frog told them. "I've tangled with Megalodon a bunch of times. He and his fellow fish aren't so hard to defeat. Sharks invading Swindon while I'm away is one thing. But now that I'm here to defend the city, I think the tables are turned."

The Amazing Frog continued to scan the horizon with his binoculars.

The better part of the day passed, and there was still no sign of Megalodon and the other sharks.

"My stomach's starting to growl," said Pig Newton. "And there are no scraps up here at the top of this skyscraper. Maybe I ought to climb back down for a while, just to find some dinner."

Suddenly, a frog opened the rooftop door and joined them on the top of the building.

"Amazing Frog!" it cried. "I saw a shark!"

The Amazing Frog was stunned.

"How is that possible?" the Amazing Frog asked. "I've been keeping an eye trained in the direction of Swindon-on-Sea this entire time, and I haven't seen a thing. Plus, we made a big barrier of parked cars all around the city, which should block any sharks from getting in."

"Are you *sure* you saw a shark?" asked Pig Newton carefully. "There are plenty of fish that look like sharks, but aren't sharks. I, personally, used to be scared of all fish everywhere until somebody explained to me that not all of them are sharks."

"It's definitely a shark," said the newly-arrived frog. "And it's *inside* the barrier of cars."

"What?" said the Amazing Frog.

"Come and see if you don't believe me!" the frog said.

The Amazing Frog followed the other frog back down the winding staircase that led down from the top of the building. When they reached the street level, they were greeted by a very unexpected sight. The Amazing Frog could hardly believe his eyes.

All over the city—*inside* their barricade of cars—were sharks! The sharks were flopping around on the asphalt and chasing people around. Some of them were even inside of buildings, poking their scary-looking heads out of doorways. It was complete chaos. Frogs were throwing their hands in the air and running around to and fro. (Frogs did this a lot anyway, whether or not there were sharks in the city. But this time, it was *definitely* due to the presence of the sharks.) And in the middle of it all—sunning himself in a parking lot in the middle of town—was a very satisfied-looking Megalodon. He had a kiddie swimming pool beside him, and every few moments one of his subordinate sharks would ladle some water over him to keep him hydrated.

"Chase them!" Megalodon shouted to his cronies. "Herd them back to Swindon-on-Sea. These frogs aren't going to get away *that* easily."

How had this happened? The Amazing Frog was furious, and he wanted answers. As he looked around in annoyance, he saw someone who he thought might have them.

Running down the street—away from one group of sharks, but toward another—was the Frog King. His crown had gotten crooked from all his running, but the Amazing Frog couldn't fail to recognize him. The Frog King had lived in Swindon longer than anybody—which may have been why he called himself king—and he would probably have answers to the questions that were now running through the Amazing Frog's head.

"Hey, Frog King," the Amazing Frog called. "Stop and talk to me a second! I know I'm always making fun of you—and saying you're just a weirdo in a crown—but this is serious. I need your help!"

"Can't you see I'm running?!" the Frog King said in exasperation. "And monarchs aren't made for running. We're made for sitting on comfy, high-backed thrones and saying 'Off with his head' and stuff. Except I'm a very kind Frog King, so I never say that. Also, I don't have a throne. But I do like to order a drink at Frog Milk Coffee and then just sit there and drink it all day. It's like my throne. Sometimes they ask me to leave after a few hours, but not always."

The Amazing Frog took an exasperated deep breath.

"You've lived here longer than anybody. Do you know how these sharks could have gotten inside the center of the city? I thought our perimeter of parked cars was going to keep them out for a while."

"Oh," said the Frog King, as if the question had not occurred to him. "I expect they came here through the sewer system. You know—the big pipes that run along the bottom of the city and bring us fresh water all the way from Swindon-on-Sea. I suppose sharks could travel through those pipes too. They're very big pipes. Even Megalodon could probably fit inside."

The Amazing Frog felt exasperated.

"And were you ever planning to tell anybody about that!?!?" he asked.

"I didn't think I needed to," said the Frog King. "I thought *you* had things all figured out!"

The Amazing Frog felt frustrated. His face fell. How could he have been so stupid as to overlook pipes under the city. And now Megalodon was here, in town!

Beside him, Pig Newton saw the Amazing Frog's sad expression and became worried.

"Oh no!" said Pig Newton. "This is the end, isn't it? We're doomed. Oh well. Swindon had a good run. Maybe I can find a new place to hang out when I'm tired of wallowing in mud."

The Amazing Frog's frown grew, but for a different reason.

"Pig Newton," the Amazing Frog began, "I love you man, but you give up way too quickly. An important part of life is not giving up, even when it looks like things are stacked against you, and even when you don't see a solution to your problem."

"It is?" asked the pig.

The Amazing Frog nodded.

"Yes. We've got a tough problem to solve right now—and things might look bad—but there's always a way to find some sort of solution. I'd like to challenge you to become part of the solution. I'd like to challenge you to not give up, and to see what happens if you try to resist even in the face of what looks like a really difficult situation. If you do, I think you'll be pleasantly surprised. And after all, what have you got to lose?"

"Hmm," said Pig Newton, thinking hard about it. "I suppose you do have a point. If we just give up on Swindon, then we lose it anyway. And I don't want that to happen. I like Swindon. If there's even a small chance of saving it, I suppose we might as well take that chance."

A smile returned to the Amazing Frog's face. He had made his friend see the light. Pig Newton did not always realize things very quickly (if he realized them at all), so this was an encouraging development!

Now there was just one important task left: Kicking these darn sharks out of Swindon for good!

A thought occurred to the Amazing Frog. It made his smile even brighter.

"What?" said Pig Newton. "Did you think of a way you could get rid of Megalodon and the sharks."

"Actually, I don't think *I* can do that," said the Amazing Frog. "But I believe I know *someone* who can!"

## Chapter Ten

There was a hush in the air far above the city of Swindon. As the sharks created chaos down below, a mysterious masked figure stepped out from behind a pillar at the top of a skyscraper. He wore a blue mask over his eyes, blue gloves, a black and yellow superhero suit, and bright blue boots. It was Batfrog, and he was here to save the day!

Sharks were known for their fear of bats generally, and of Batfrog in particular. Bats were scary for sharks because they could fly over and annoy you—or even bite you—and then fly up into the sky where you could never get revenge. (As you might imagine, getting revenge was very important for sharks.) Bats were also small and could often fit between a shark's giant teeth. That made getting revenge hard too. Bats were also not afraid of sharks. This might have annoyed sharks most of all. Perhaps it was because sharks' enormous, gaping mouths reminded bats of welcoming caves, which was where they usually lived. And the giant teeth reminded them of stalactites and stalagmites. Whatever the case, bats buzzed sharks with no fear.

A frog crossed with a bat was likewise a problem for sharks. It combined the reckless bravery of a bat with the annoyingness of a frog. Also, even though bats were a problem, sharks didn't much want to eat them. They were stringy and didn't have much meat. Frogs, on the other hand, were delicious and sharks always wanted to eat them. That meant it was twice as annoying when you *couldn't* eat them. What a drag!

Batfrog looked out across Swindon. His uniform flapped dramatically in the wind. As chaos erupted below and sharks chased frogs down the streets of the city, he remained an unflappable statue. Eventually, one of the frogs glanced up and noticed.

"Look up there!" the frog cried.

"What is it?" asked another frog. "Is it a bird? Is it a plane? Is it a frog in a Halloween costume?"

"Dude, it's Batfrog!" said another. "*He'll* know what to do!"

In truth, Batfrog was still figuring it out. This was because Batfrog was actually the Amazing Frog in a special suit. But that's not to say there was no difference between Batfrog and the Amazing Frog. Every time he put on that suit, the Amazing Frog felt something special come over him. It was like he was becoming a different person. Everything about him was amplified. This included his desire to do crazy things, and to mess with sharks. Luckily for the city of Swindon, this was exactly what was called for at this very moment.

Batfrog—which was what the Amazing Frog always called himself in the suit—knew that the best course of action was often to just jump right in. So faced with this latest crisis, that was what he did. Literally.

Batfrog flung himself off of the building and aimed for a car below. It was a big yellow station wagon with a roof that looked especially springy. Batfrog hit it head on and used the momentum to spring up even higher than he had been before. From that height, he could get an even better view of the sharks terrorizing Swindon.

Batfrog began to drift back down again. This time, he aimed for a bright blue sports car. He hit it right on the hood. The rebound lifted him once again into the stratosphere high above the city.

Batfrog took another look below. Finally, in the very center of the city, he spied Megalodon. The giant shark was looking around at the worried, fleeing frogs and smiling an evil smile. His eyes looked even more insane than usual. (They always looked a little bit insane.) Batfrog could see that Megalodon was angry at having been fooled during their Olympic events. Now he wanted revenge.

Batfrog bounced off of another car and thought about a plan of attack. For some superheroes, a "plan of attack" was an expression of how you were going to proceed. But for Batfrog, it was literal. He was going to attack Megalodon. Now it was just a matter of figuring out the best way.

Sometimes the best answer was the most straightforward one. Like lasers coming straight off a laser gun. With this in mind, Batfrog pulled his laser gun out of his trousers and arced himself in the direction of Megalodon.

"Hey Megalodon!" Batfrog cried as he flew closer to the giant shark. "Open wide!"

"Huh?" said Megalodon. He looked around for where the voice was coming from. Then, at the last moment, he looked upwards just as Batfrog soared past. As he did, Batfrog pointed his laser gun at Megalodon and pulled the trigger.

A bright light shot out and hit Megalodon right in his gaping mouth.

The giant shark did not appear in the least annoyed by this development. His smile grew even brighter.

"Ahh, thank you Batfrog," said Megalodon. "I'd had something stuck between my teeth for a week. You finally got it out. We sharks don't have arms, so a good dentist is essential. Even an unofficial one, who dresses up like a bat!"

Batfrog was annoyed that the laser hadn't worked, but he was not about to give up. He landed on another car, and bounced high into the sky. He pulled a different weapon out of his suit. This time it was a crossbow. Batfrog took aim. He was careful to adjust for his trajectory through the air, wind resistance, and his own farting. When he had a good bead on Megalodon's face, he let the crossbow bolt fly.

It shot right toward Megalodon's mouth. With one skillful bite, the shark caught it in its teeth.

"Ahh, a toothpick!" the shark said. "Just the thing I need to continue my dental cleaning. Thank you for providing it, Batfrog."

Megalodon grinned evilly, the crossbow bolt protruding.

Batfrog was 0-2. He realized he needed a new approach, and fast. Batfrog knew that where Megalodon went, the other sharks would follow. If he could just get rid of Megalodon, the other sharks would leave the city. Still, it looked like attacking Megalodon with conventional weapons wasn't going to work. But there had to be another way!

Batfrog looked down for another car to land on. That was when he saw something that changed everything.

On the other side of the parking lot where Megalodon was holding court, there was a long yellow school bus. Immediately, a plan hatched inside of Batfrog's brain. He began to calculate what would be needed to set it into action.

Batfrog came down on another car (being careful to avoid the school bus) and bounced high back into the air. As he flew, he pulled yet another weapon from his stash. It was his good old rocket launcher. Down below him, Megalodon narrowed his eyes.

Batfrog took careful aim with the rocket launcher and let the missile fly. It was clear from the trajectory that it was not going to hit Megalodon. The missile would land a foot or two in front of him. Even Megalodon noticed this.

"Ha ha!" the giant shark just had time to say. "You missed!"

Then the projectile explosive struck the pavement. The resulting blast sent Megalodon flying high into the air. He spun head-over-tail, and thrashed wildly as he did.

"Oh," Batfrog said thoughtfully. "I don't think I missed at all."

"Ahhh," Megalodon shrieked. "What's happening? What did you do? Sharks aren't meant to spin through the air!"

"Relax," Batfrog called. "It'll all be over soon."

It was.

A moment later, Megalodon landed with a great THUD atop the long yellow school bus. Batfrog had been concerned that Megalodon's weight might crush the bus, but the vehicle had held together. It even looked drivable. Which was good, because driving the bus was the next part of Batfrog's plan.

Batfrog made his own landing on the parking lot. He picked himself up as quickly as he could and raced on his little froggy legs toward the bus. He threw open the driver's side door and climbed inside. Megalodon was still disoriented and had obviously hit his head hard. He didn't understand what was happening. Batfrog turned on the ignition and stepped on the gas before Megalodon was aware that he was on top of a bus.

"What. . . what's going on?" Megalodon cried in a disoriented haze. "Why are the buildings around me moving? What's going on?"

"You're just having a dream," Batfrog called from behind the wheel. "Close your eyes and go back to sleep."

"Oh, okay. . ." Megalodon said fuzzily.

Then something occurred to the enormous fish.

"Waaaaait," it said. "Sharks sleep with our eyes open. We don't close our eyes to sleep. We only close our eyes to protect them when we're going after prey. . . like yummy delicious frogs."

"Well, are your eyes open right now?" Batfrog asked.

"Yes," Megalodon answered.

"So then you must be dreaming," Batfrog explained.

"Oh. . ." Megalodon said dreamily. "I guess you're right."

Batfrog pushed down on the bus's gas pedal and drove as fast as he could. Unfortunately, with the enormous shark weighing down the bus, that wasn't very fast at all. The bus moved at a pace that would—for most people—be close to a light jog.

As Batfrog made his way toward the edge of Swindon, he saw a familiar face by the side of the road.

"Hey, Pig Newton," Batfrog called, rolling down the window. "Hop on board."

For a moment, Pig Newton was startled at the sight of Batfrog driving Megalodon down the street on the back of a school bus. Then Pig Newton remembered all of the unusual things he had seen in the past 24 hours or so, and decided that maybe this wasn't really so strange after all. He began running alongside the bus.

"Can you go a little slower?" Pig Newton puffed. "I'm not a jogging kind of animal. I'm more of a standing-around animal."

Batfrog slowed the bus for a moment and opened the door for passengers. Pig Newton caught up and quickly climbed inside. Then Batfrog hit the gas again, and sent the bus surging forward. Pig Newton scuttled around to get a foothold in the aisle.

"What are you doing?" Pig Newton asked. "Why is Megalodon on the back of a bus?"

"It's simple," Batfrog answered. "We're taking him back where he belongs. And when he's gone, the other sharks won't know what to do. They'll be powerless and leaderless. Look out of the back of the bus if you want to see what I mean."

Pig Newton warily crept to the back of the bus and glanced out the rear window. All at once, he realized that Batfrog was right! The other sharks who had invaded the city had stopped chasing the frogs. Instead, they were looking on in confusion. With their leader incapacitated and leaving on a bus, they didn't know what to do. They began shrinking back into the sewers and diving into the manholes that would take them to the underground pipes leading back to Swindon-on-Sea.

"Hey, you're right!" Pig Newton said. "They're all leaving. Yay!"

But Pig Newton abruptly cut himself off mid-cheer as a dark possibility occurred to him.

"Wait a second," he said. "If we take Megalodon back to Swindon-on-Sea, then all the other sharks will meet him there. Then they might outnumber us. That could be very bad."

"Did I *say* we were going to Swindon-on-Sea?" Batfrog asked with a twinkle in his eye.

"Um. . . no," answered Pig Newton. "But then. . . but then. . . Where *are* we going?"

"It's a place you already know," Batfrog said. He offered no other details, and simply continued driving out of town. Behind the school bus the last of the sharks slinked away out of view. Soon, it was only frogs again in Swindon. When they realized what had happened, the frogs began to raise their hands and cheer. Even frogs who were normally very grumpy took the time to celebrate. They continued cheering as Batfrog drove the bus carrying Megalodon over the horizon and out of sight.

Whether there was any relationship between the Amazing Frog and Batfrog was not something that had ever been totally clear to Pig Newton. He had his hunches and suspicions, but had never come right out and asked about it. He was pretty sure they were the same person, but he didn't want to be wrong on such an important thing. That would be embarrassing. True, he had never seen the Amazing Frog and Batfrog in the same place at the same time, but there was still room for doubt in his mind.

Because of this doubt, Pig Newton chose his words carefully when a big, J-shaped building began to loom into view on the horizon.

"That's Joke Frog's castle!" Pig Newton said. "Or rather, the castle Megalodon wanted us to believe was Joke Frog's castle. I recognize it because I saw it earlier today. And maybe you have seen it before too? Maybe?"

Batfrog gave Pig Newton the smallest grin.

"The castle *is* our destination," Batfrog said neutrally. "It just so happens that I'm going to give Megalodon a taste of his own medicine."

"Oh," replied Pig Newton. "That doesn't sound very nice. Medicine always tastes very bad to me. In fact, I only take it when a doctor tells me to. But maybe that's the idea."

Batfrog pulled the bus up to the front of the castle and got out. Megalodon was still on top of the bus, and still looked quite dazed. While he was still in this harmless state, Batfrog gripped Megalodon by the tail and began—very slowly—to pull him down from the bus.

"You want to lend a hand. . . or a hoof?" Batfrog asked Pig Newton.

"Oh," the pig said. "I would but. . . That's Megalodon. I'm still pretty scared of him."

"In that case, could you at least get the door?" Batfrog asked. "I don't think it's locked."

"Okay," Pig Newton said, relieved he did not need to get close enough to touch Megalodon.

As Pig Newton threw the door to the castle wide open, Batfrog got Megalodon off of the bus and began pulling him inside. It was slow going. Megalodon looked around with a strange smile, seeming to enjoy the ride.

"Am I still dreaming?" the concussed shark asked. "What is this?"

"Wait a bit longer and you'll find out," Batfrog assured him.

Once Megalodon was through the castle door, Batfrog turned again to Pig Newton.

"Now we need to lift that cage and put Megalodon inside!" Batfrog said.

"No problem!" said Pig Newton, strapping himself into the harness. "And I won't even need extra motor-vation this time. After what Megalodon has done, I've got all that I need. If ever anybody needed to be inside a cage, it's him!"

Pig Newton strained as hard as he could in the harness and lifted the heavy cage high into the air. Batfrog dragged the disoriented shark directly underneath and stepped away.

"Okay," he said. "Let the cage fall."

Pig Newton lowered the cage down on top of Megalodon.

"Serves him right for all the frogs he tricked," Pig Newton said. "But now what do we do?"

"Megalodon is long overdue for a talking-to," said Batfrog. "But he needs to regain his wits for that to be effective. Otherwise, he'll think it was all a dream. So for the moment. . . we wait."

Pig Newton explored the castle while they waited for Megalodon to feel more like himself again. (Really, this meant waiting for him to become much nastier, because the giant shark was really very nasty.) As he explored the castle, Pig Newton couldn't help but think that it had the potential to be a very nice place—provided you weren't stuck in a cage while you were in it. If you painted the walls and hung some nice art and improved the lighting situation, then instead of being dank and scary it might be the kind of place a person might very much enjoy living. Pig Newton hoped the castle could be repurposed somehow after all of this foolishness with Megalodon had ended!

After several hours of exploring, Pig Newton noticed that Megalodon was seeming much more like himself.

"Ooh, my head!" Megalodon cried. "I feel like someone blew me into the air with a rocket launcher!"

"You feel that way because that's exactly what happened to you," said a familiar voice.

Out of the shadows strolled the Amazing Frog. Pig Newton looked around and noticed that Batfrog was now nowhere to be found! The switch had happened again. . . but Pig Newton hadn't seen it happen, so he still couldn't say *for sure* that the Amazing Frog and Batfrog were the same frog! Pig Newton resolved to be more observant in the future.

Inside the cage, Megalodon shook his head as if trying to rouse himself from a deep slumber.

"Oof," said the shark. "So then it *wasn't* a dream? And neither was being dragged here on the back of a school bus?"

"That wasn't a dream either," said the Amazing Frog.

"Darn it!" said Megalodon. "None of my plans have worked out! This is the worst!"

"It's maybe the worst for *you*," the Amazing Frog pointed out. "But it's not so bad for all of the poor frogs you were trying to capture, harass, and eat."

"To be honest . . . capturing, harassing, and eating frogs are like ninety percent of my plans," Megalodon admitted. "Maybe ninety-five, actually."

"Whatever the case, we need to have a serious talk," the Amazing Frog told him. "These latest plots of yours have gone too far. It's one thing when you terrorize frogs who choose to go swimming in Swindon-on-Sea. Those frogs know what they're getting into, and it's a risk they're willing to take. But when you come after Swindon itself. . . well, you've crossed a line, Megalodon."

"I'm sorry," said the giant shark. "I just get envious and greedy. And hungry. For frogs."

"Even so, what you did was too much," the Amazing Frog continued. "We're going to have to talk about what we can do to ensure it doesn't happen again in the future."

"Or what?" Megalodon said in an angry, confrontational way. It was clear he was getting back to his former self.

"Or you can stay in this cage—which *you* built—and think about what you've done!" the Amazing Frog said, and crossed his skinny arms.

Megalodon frowned. It was clear that sitting in a cage for ages and ages didn't seem like it would be very desirable at all.

"Okay," said Megalodon. "From now on I'll limit my frog-eating activities to Swindon-on-Sea! I promise! Now let me out of this cage!"

"I'd *like* to believe you," said the Amazing Frog. "But how can I know for certain that you're really and truly a changed shark? You could be fibbing because you know it's what I want to hear."

"Fibbing?" said Megalodon. "I'm not fibbing. I promise!"

The Amazing Frog looked Megalodon up and down, as if he were trying to make a difficult determination.

"No," the Amazing Frog said. "I think we're going to need you to *demonstrate* that you've changed your ways."

Megalodon's eyes went back and forth nervously.

"Demonstrate?" the shark asked. "How am I supposed to do that?"

"Oh, I've got an idea," said the Amazing Frog. "Actually, I think you'll like it. It involves violence and breaking things."

"I do like violence and breaking things," Megalodon admitted.

"In that case, I'll tell you more," the Amazing Frog said. He crept close to the cage and began to whisper into one of the tiny holes that served as Megalodon's ears.

Megalodon's eyes grew even larger than usual, and his mouth dropped open.

"But. . . But. . ." sputtered Megalodon. "If we do that. . ."

Megalodon drew his ear away from the cage and turned to look the Amazing Frog squarely in the face.

"If we do that, then my entire dastardly plot has been for nothing!" Megalodon whined.

The Amazing Frog began to feel frustrated with the giant shark. Surely, what Megalodon was now describing was indeed the point of the exercise.

"Well, if you'd rather stay in the cage, I *suppose* Pig Newton and I could go do it ourselves, without you" the Amazing Frog said, turning around and making a beeline for the castle door. "Come on, Pig Newton. Megalodon doesn't want to help. I guess we'll have to go and do fun, adventurous, violent stuff—with lots of cool explosions—without him."

"Nooooo," cried Megalodon. "Don't do that! If you're gonna do it anyway, I should at least get to be there for it!"

The Amazing Frog paused mid-step. Pig Newton looked up at him questioningly. The Amazing Frog gave Pig Newton a wink. They had done it!

"Okay," the Amazing Frog said, turning back around. "If you're sure."

"Yes, I'm sure," cried the shark. "Just let me out of this cage!"

"You'll have to ride on the school bus again," the Amazing Frog warned him. "Are you going to be all right with that?"

"Anything, anything!" cried Megalodon.

The Amazing Frog smiled.

"Okay," he said. "Pig Newton, lift the cage again. I think our friend has learned his lesson."

"Oh, I have; I certainly have!" Megalodon said as Pig Newton once more stepped into the harness and lifted the cage up to the roof of the castle.

The Amazing Frog prepared to pull Megalodon by the tail again, but the giant shark seemed keen to move under his own power. He began using his fins to flop back and forth and to push himself across the castle floor. In this way, Megalodon walked himself out of the castle and back to the school bus.

"I might need a little help getting on top of it again," Megalodon admitted. "Sharks aren't very good at climbing."

"Sure thing," said the Amazing Frog.

Megalodon suddenly closed his eyes and gritted his teeth. His expression said that he anticipated some horrible, surprising pain at any moment.

"What's with him?" Pig Newton asked, emerging from the castle.

"I think he think's I'm going to blast him with a rocket launcher again," the Amazing Frog said with a laugh.

Megalodon opened one eye, cautiously.

"Well. . . aren't you?" the shark said.

"I had to use the rocket launcher back in Swindon because you were busy being a jerk!" the Amazing Frog explained. "Now that you've agreed to be nice—or *nicer,* at least—I think Pig Newton and I can just push you up to the top of the bus with our hands."

"Ahh!" said Megalodon, his frightened expression falling away. "That sounds much better than being blasted with a rocket launcher. Let's definitely do it that way!"

Summoning all their strength, the Amazing Frog and Pig Newton positioned themselves at the side of Megalodon and began to lift him up to the roof of the bus. It was slow going. Megalodon was very heavy.

"Urrgh," the Amazing Frog grunted. "Put your back into it, Pig Newton."

"I *am*!" said the pig. "And I'm mostly back! I don't have much of a neck. So really, I'm putting most of *me* into it."

Megalodon's great bulk hovered near the roof of the bus.

"Megalodon, can you help too?" asked the Amazing Frog.

"Oh, sorry," the shark said. "I thought I was supposed to let you guys do this."

Megalodon used his fins to get a hold on the top of the bus, and then rolled over onto it. Soon, he was sitting squarely on the roof once more. Pig Newton and the Amazing Frog breathed a great sigh of relief.

The Amazing Frog and Pig Newton climbed into the bus. The Amazing Frog got behind the wheel and started to drive. The bus shuddered under Megalodon's weight, but managed to get started. The Amazing Frog turned the bus around and headed for the coast.

"We're going to Swindon-on-Sea?" asked Pig Newton.

The Amazing Frog nodded.

"What are we going to do when we get there?" Pig Newton pressed.

"Oh, you'll see," the Amazing Frog said cryptically. "It'll be a little test for Megalodon. We'll find out if he's really changed his ways."

Pig Newton wondered what this could mean. He rode in silence the rest of the way, but his mind was quite active. He was trying to think of something that Megalodon could do to prove he wasn't going to be a jerk anymore. Not only could Pig Newton not visualize such a test, he couldn't visualize Megalodon passing it!

Eventually, the school bus pulled up at the edge of Swindon-on-Sea and came to a halt. There was the dock, the familiar parked watercraft, and the remains of the half-built fake Swindon that Megalodon had been forcing the frogs to construct. The bay was also full of sharks. They had apparently given up on their assault on Swindon, and had returned to the water.

The Amazing Frog opened the door of the bus and hopped out.

"Okay," he said to Megalodon. "Remember what we talked about. I want to see lots of enthusiasm!"

"I know, I know," said the enormous shark. Megalodon shuffled his enormous bulk off the side of the bus and plopped back onto the ground. Then he duck-walked (or shark-walked) on his fins until he reached the edge of the water. Megalodon slithered beneath the waves and disappeared.

The Amazing Frog waited. He didn't say anything, but he knew that this was the true test. Nothing would stop Megalodon from swimming out to sea and ignoring their agreement entirely. The shark was a known jerk, and going back on a promise would not be the worst thing he'd done in the last few hours.

Yet the Amazing Frog was relieved—and pleasantly surprised—when Megalodon's giant head re-emerged from the water moments later. The huge head turned toward the Amazing Frog.

"All right," said Megalodon. "I'm a shark of my word. Where do we begin?"

When it came to causing chaos and destroying things, the Amazing Frog was the best around. He could jump on cars and obliterate them. He could explode things with explosives and rocket launchers. He could also use smaller arms—like, say, machine guns and laser guns—to destroy things a bit more gradually. But the point was, *they got destroyed.*

Megalodon, on the other hand, was skilled at destroying yummy delicious frogs with his teeth, but most of his destruction of property was *incidental.* He might break a watercraft in the course of trying to eat the frog who was riding it, but the watercraft was never his goal.

This was what the Amazing Frog was about to change.

The Amazing Frog looked out across the half-built city in the bay. Then he pulled a rocket launcher out of his inventory and took aim at a partially-erected skyscraper peeking out from the water. He squeezed the trigger and shot the missile directly at the structure. It burst into rocky bits and a hail of rubble splashed into the sea all around them.

"Now you," the Amazing Frog said to Megalodon.

"But I don't have a rocket launcher," the enormous fish complained.

"Yeah," said the Amazing Frog. "But you *do* have being a giant shark the size of a house. Try taking a run at that building over there. Really put your weight into it!"

Obediently, Megalodon backed up a few feet, then dove beneath the water and launched himself like a torpedo at one of the half-built buildings. As the shark connected, it seemed as though the entire bay shook. Bricks exploded everywhere. The structure fell over and sank into the water.

"Erm, what are we doing exactly?" Pig Newton whispered to the Amazing Frog.

The Amazing Frog grinned.

"If Megalodon is serious about abandoning his plan to build his own city in Swindon-on-Sea, then he won't mind destroying it. Helping us out is a great way for him to prove he's changed his ways."

At that moment, Megalodon's bulky head emerged again from the water.

"How'd I do?" Megalodon asked.

"You did great," the Amazing Frog said. "That building got totally obliterated. Think you can do it again?"

"*Can* I?" the shark said enthusiastically. "Just watch this!"

And the shark disappeared underneath the water again. Only a single fin was visible. As the Amazing Frog and Pig Newton watched, that fin got up to ramming speed and headed straight for another partially-built structure. There was an enormous sonic BOOM! From underneath the water as Megalodon crashed into it. Bits of brick fell like a hailstorm from the sky. When the dust and falling debris cleared, there was no sign of the building anymore.

"Excellent work!" the Amazing Frog said as Megalodon reemerged from the sea. "You're a natural at this. You're born to do it."

"Hmm," said the giant shark. "I never tried ramming into things and destroying them before. It's kind of fun! I'm not sure it's as fun as catching frogs, but it's certainly up there."

"Want to do it some more?" the Amazing Frog asked expectantly.

"Absolutely!" Megalodon cried, and plunged once more beneath the waves. Pretty soon, all of the major structures in the bay were falling one, after the other. All the Amazing Frog had to do was stand back and watch.

"This is awesome!" said Pig Newton. "Megalodon is doing our work for us!  I never thought this would happen!"

"See how things can go when you keep trying and don't give up?" the Amazing Frog replied.

"I certainly do!" said Pig Newton. "They can go great, and really awesome things can happen. Like Megalodon doing your work for you!"

Then a thought suddenly occurred to Pig Newton, and he became introspective.

"Do you think this means Megalodon is our friend now, and won't try to eat us and stuff?"

"I wouldn't go that far," said the Amazing Frog. "I bet he'll still try to eat us whenever we jump in the sea. But he certainly won't try to take over Swindon or its residents again. I think we've made sure of that!"

And so—as the structures in the bay continued to fall crashing into the water—the Amazing Frog and Pig Newton headed back home, confident that they had saved Swindon. They knew that it was all but certain that Megalodon would get up to *some* kind of trouble again soon. But they also knew that they would be there to stop him!

**THE END**

Printed in Great Britain
by Amazon

# The Quest to Save Swindon

## An Unofficial Amazing Frog Adventure

By Pungence
with Scott Kenemore

**ISBN-13: 978-1542566773**

**ISBN-10: 1542566770**